She'd

She was honest. Direct. She hadn't pulled any punches. It was as if she didn't have time for games, and that was fine with him. He had long ago become frustrated with so many of the women he'd met since his divorce.

Burt could envision her clearly now, in his mind's eye, standing by her bike. Her skin had felt warm and smooth when he'd touched her chin. He'd wanted to touch her hair; it had looked so soft in the dusky evening air.

At that moment, he'd realized he wanted— needed—to feel close to someone again.

Not someone. Sandy.

He hadn't felt excited by life in such a long time. Now a woman with shimmering hair, steady gray-blue eyes and a totally spontaneous smile had burst into his life and turned it upside down. For the longest time he'd felt he'd had walls built up around his heart. But Sandy had started to scale those walls when he hadn't been looking. And in the end all that mattered was that he was happy when he was with her.

Sandy. He thought of her. And smiled.

ABOUT THE AUTHOR

Elda Minger became a writer via a circuitous route. Through the years she has worked in several bookstores—where an early Woodiwiss novel got her interested in romances—cleaned houses in Beverly Hills, ushered in theaters, sung for her supper on Hollywood Boulevard and even appeared in two movies. Born in and now residing again in Hollywood, Elda has lived in many parts of the United States as well as in foreign countries.

Books by Elda Minger

HARLEQUIN AMERICAN ROMANCE

Don't miss any of our special offers. Write to us at the following address for information on our newest releases.

Harlequin Reader Service
901 Fuhrmann Blvd., P.O. Box 1397, Buffalo, NY 14240
Canadian address: P.O. Box 603,
Fort Erie, Ont. L2A 5X3

Nothing in Common
Elda Minger

Harlequin Books

TORONTO • NEW YORK • LONDON
AMSTERDAM • PARIS • SYDNEY • HAMBURG
STOCKHOLM • ATHENS • TOKYO • MILAN

To Paul and Aline Monroe,
cherished uncle and aunt,
for so much love and support;
and to Barbara Bretton.
You were the best part of the journey.

Published January 1988

First printing November 1987

ISBN 0-373-16229-4

Chapter One

The grenade hit the wall, bounced off and rolled into the far corner of the alley.

Burt Thomson glared at the green letters on his computer screen and let out a disgusted sigh.

"That's just terrific," he muttered.

His fingers typed rapidly, and the glowing letters on the screen shifted and changed.

Grenade! It hit the brick surface, glanced off and bounced into the dark alley. Savage knew he had mere seconds before—

He sighed again, this time raking his fingers impatiently through the dark thickness of his hair.

Before what? he thought disgustedly.

Another day, another writer's block.

You have minus eighty-three days before this manuscript has to be turned in. You are getting absolutely nothing done. Your writing has never sunk to levels like this before.

He pondered what his fictional character Jack Savage would do. Jack was usually never short of inventive, though violent, solutions. Burt smiled, leaned back in his chair and closed his eyes.

"You have a contract with us, Mr. Savage," the editor said softly, rolling the pencil between his fleshy palms. *"And I think you know what we do with people who fail to honor their contracts."*

Savage scanned the room with icy gray eyes. There was only one way he could escape. Straight through that pile of manuscripts and out the front door past the receptionist. His fingers itched as he felt for the pin of the grenade. It was a drastic measure, but the only one available.

The grenade hit the manuscripts.

Amid anguished cries, he darted through the smoke and flying manuscript pages, determined to get out at any cost. . . .

Burt's eyes snapped open. *Buddy, you have a major problem.*

He straightened in his chair and returned his attention to the screen. Taking a deep breath, he forced himself to type.

All three of the men in the alley recognized it immediately.

Grenade!

The grenade exploded with a thunderous roar, and Savage felt the fury of the blast as it ripped through the—

"Daddy."

The tremulous, high-pitched voice caught his attention at once. Turning, Burt saw his younger son, Ryan, standing in the doorway, his hand on the knob.

"Ryan, I thought I told you—"

"I *did* knock, Daddy, but you didn't hear me. Cici is real mad. She says this time Wadsworth—"

"Cici? Wadsworth? Ryan, what—"

"It's her damn flowers," his son said, his dark blue eyes watching his father's face for any sign of a reaction.

"Don't say damn," Burt said automatically. He was already on his feet, headed out the door and toward the backyard. Ryan followed, close on his heels.

Outside, all was pandemonium.

Cecilia Forrest, their next-door neighbor, was down in the dirt with Wadsworth, Ryan's English sheepdog. The dog had a clump of brilliantly colored lilies in his mouth, his rump wiggling as he dug in his massive paws and played tug-of-war. Cici, her face flushed, was shredding their stems, battling for possession.

Burt was astonished for just an instant. Cici, cool and blond and regal, classy Cici, down in the dirt with a dog. Cici, who never had so much as a pleat out of place.

"Give me those lilies, you— Oh, Burt, Wadsworth is just too strong for me! He jumped into my yard while I was gardening, and—"

"Wadsworth, drop it!"

The sheepdog recognized his master's voice. He let go of the lilies, sending Cici sprawling, then darted away, crashing into the bushes behind Cici's house.

"Cici, I'm sorry." Burt jumped the low fence separating their properties and ran over to his neighbor, offering her a hand up.

"Oh, Burt." Her pale blue eyes were full of tears, and her chin quivered. "I know that dog is important to your children, but he—he frightens me."

If there was one thing Burt couldn't stand, it was seeing a woman cry. He felt his insides twisting, remembering all the times Anne's eyes had filled and she'd retreated to their bedroom to sob in silence.

He had always felt so guilty.

"Cici," he said softly as he held her trembling form against his chest. "I promise you, this time I'll do something about Wadsworth."

WITHIN THE HOUR, Wadsworth was locked in Ryan's bedroom, and Burt and his younger son were seated in the den. Michael, his oldest, was lying on one of the sofas, the remote control in his hands as he flipped through the channels.

"Daddy, are you going to send Wadsworth away?" Ryan asked.

"No," Burt said, hating the uncertain look on the five-year-old's face. When he and Anne had divorced eighteen months ago, he had known it was going to do terrible things to their children. Anne had wanted time to find herself. He had insisted on custody of Michael and Ryan, and had kept the house. It hadn't been an act of cruelty on his part—Anne hadn't wanted any encumbrances in her life's master plan. He'd tried his best to give his sons a sense of security, and the knowledge that the divorce had had nothing to do with either of them.

He and Anne should never have married in the first place.

Only two good things had come out of their marriage, and both of them were here in the den with him.

"C'mere." He patted the couch cushion next to him, and Ryan launched his sturdy little body toward him. Michael glanced over at the two of them for a second, then returned his attention to the television.

"Dad, you should just get rid of—"

"No! Michael, no—" Ryan's voice rose as he panicked.

"Hey! Hey! Michael, that's enough. There's a solution to this, and it doesn't have to be giving Wadsworth away. If we all think hard enough, something's sure to come up."

Burt closed his eyes and leaned his head back against the soft leather of the sofa. He felt Ryan's head come to rest against his chest, and he tightened his arm around his son. Ryan had always been more of a toucher, more emotional. Michael was the one he worried about. His older son had been so terribly quiet throughout the entire divorce proceedings. He had watched his mother back her car out of the driveway that final time with his facial expression frozen in place and his spine ramrod stiff.

He had been eight years old.

"Do you have an idea, Daddy?" Ryan's voice piped up.

"Nope. But I'm working on it."

"We could build Wadsworth a house in the back and keep him locked up," Michael suggested.

"Michael, no, I don't want—"

"Michael, come on. I'm looking for a constructive solution."

A short silence ensued. Burt glanced over at Michael, noticing the tightness around the boy's mouth. His older son had rarely been deliberately mean as a child. But in the past year he'd come to pick on his younger brother more and more. Burt put a stop to it when he could catch him at it, but it hurt him to see Michael suffer. And take it out on Ryan.

"Maybe...maybe we could send Cici on a long vacation, and then she wouldn't have to see Wadsworth." Ryan looked up hopefully.

"Great idea, baby face," Michael said, his voice sarcastic.

"I am not a baby—"

"Michael, enough." Burt's voice was quiet, but the message it contained was quite clear. He'd never believed in raising his voice or spanking as a means of discipline. His own parents had done a fine job without resorting to any of those tactics. As Anne had drifted farther and farther away from them, he had taken over more and more of the child raising. It hadn't been easy. The world was so much more complicated than when he'd been a boy.

"Daddy, how about we—"

"How about this?" Michael abruptly turned up the sound on the television, and all attention was turned toward the image on the twenty-seven-inch color screen. A girl was walking a striking German shepherd on a long leather leash as a man's voice talked excitedly about a dog-training program.

"—in the safety and comfort of your own home. Our trainers are the best in the business, and their work is guaranteed. Imagine yourself with a dog you can be proud of, a dog you'll never have to worry about again—"

An image flashed on the screen of a shaggy dog digging furiously in a garden.

"Wadsworth!" Ryan shrieked delightedly.

"—your dog more like this? Why settle for less when you can have—"

The next image showed a small poodle jumping through a hoop.

"Wow," Ryan breathed.

"Where's a pencil?" Michael said, sitting up.

"In the desk," Burt replied, never taking his eyes off the screen. This might just be the solution he had been looking for.

"THERE'S SOME NUT on the phone with an English sheepdog that's ruining his life. He needs a trainer today. He's in the valley, in Sherman Oaks. Which one of you guys wants to take it?"

Dolores Kramden, chief receptionist for the Canine Institute of Dog Training, was a busty blonde who was partial to high heels, short skirts and outrageous sweaters. But she had a terrific phone voice and a sense of calm that spread throughout the office like the warmth of a tropical breeze.

Four pairs of eyes looked up from an assortment of desks.

"I can't on such short notice," said Marilyn, a slim brunette with short hair. "I have to go to the Christmanns' at two. Gorky is having problems adjusting to the new baby."

"Count me out." Mark looked like a classic blond surfer. "I'm due at the Corsinos' in half an hour. Their bulldog keeps attacking the garbagemen."

"Damn. I have to go see Mrs. Cunningham and her poodles." Dan's gray eyes were disappointed.

"I'll go."

Dolores frowned. "Sandy, I thought you had to be at the Cohens' this afternoon."

"I did. Mrs. Cohen doesn't believe in discipline for Desiree. She told me not to come back."

"Isn't that the dog that was ruining her carpets?"

"One and the same."

"How do we get ahold of these crazies?" Dolores rolled her eyes. "Spare me the Mrs. Cohens of this world. Okay then, I'm going to go tell this guy you're on. Can you leave right away?"

"Sure."

"Oh, and Sandy, park the motorcycle a few houses down this time. We've had a couple of complaints about it."

As Sandy Hensley maneuvered her motorcycle through the Wednesday afternoon traffic, she thought about what Dolores had told her about Burt Thomson and his dog, Wadsworth.

Burt was a writer. Even worse, a writer on a deadline. He lived in Sherman Oaks with his two sons. Wadsworth, the dog, was responsible for destroying property and various other acts of mischief.

He's probably not getting enough attention. That was the trouble with most dog owners. They put more thought into selecting a car or buying a home than in deciding whether or not they wanted a dog.

People liked the idea of a dog. Lassie. Rin Tin Tin. Slippers fetched in the evening, a wagging tail to greet them after a hard day at work. Their own private canine fan club.

No one loved you quite the way a dog did.

But the reality was housebreaking, chewed slippers, holes in the yard, jumped fences, cars chased, howling and barking. All problems that had solutions, but all problems that had to be worked on.

Time was the solution. Time, and setting definite priorities.

She wondered what Burt would look like. None of the writers she had met so far had fit the stereotype, the tweed jacket with leather patches and pipe-in-mouth look. If he was established enough to be working out of his own home, he was probably older.

But then again, you couldn't count on that. Her roommates had told her often enough that there were kids in their twenties making major decisions in the movie studios these days. Creativity didn't necessarily mean a person had to be older and wiser. Burt could be any age.

Watching traffic carefully, Sandy turned left off Ventura Boulevard and started up away from traffic. She was careful not to gun her motorcycle, remembering what Dolores had said. She wasn't going to cause a disturbance, but she'd be damned if she'd park her bike down the street.

Burt Thomson would just have to take her the way she was.

"DADDY, WHEN WILL SANDY BE HERE?" Ryan looked up at his father, his face expectant.

"Soon."

"Will she like Wadsworth?" Now Ryan sounded worried.

He knew where that question came from. The last time Anne had visited—almost three months ago—Wadsworth had jumped up on her linen suit and muddied it. She'd flown into a rage, her temper getting the best of her. Burt had often thought, especially in the last few years of his marriage, that Anne's father had done no one any favors by spoiling his only daughter.

But this trainer couldn't possibly dislike dogs. It was her job, after all. He pictured a sturdy British woman with a sensible tweed skirt and plain sweater, leather walking shoes and glasses. White hair. Twinkling blue eyes. Dog biscuits tucked in her pocket.

Wadsworth would probably love her.

"What a cool bike!" Michael's excited voice broke into his thoughts.

The motorcycle was purring smoothly up their driveway. For one moment Burt thought the rider was lost and seeking directions. If she had seen them all standing in the front yard, it would have been logical to pull up and ask.

Now, as the cyclist slowed the bike and turned off the ignition, he wasn't as sure.

All three of them watched as the rider got off her motorcycle. Gloved hands removed a helmet, and Burt tried not to stare as an explosion of strawberry-blond hair appeared.

"Hi," the blond woman said, her tone easy. "I'm Sandy, from the Canine Institute." And then she smiled.

Burt felt something tighten in his chest. She was a pretty woman, with high cheekbones, a generous mouth and steady gray-blue eyes. There was even a smattering of freckles across her face. Her nose fit her face, the end tilted just enough to give her a mischievous look.

But when she smiled... This was the woman you saw on Pepsi commercials, facing the camera, a smile lighting up her face, drinking a soft drink. Burt was surprised to find himself with a sense of expectancy, but he wasn't sure what it was he thought might happen. She looked like the sort of woman who made sure her life contained a generous dollop of fun.

She took off her gloves, then unzipped her black leather jacket. The black denims she wore were cut loosely, and the short-sleeved sweatshirt was faded and shapeless.

Her helmet, gloves and jacket safely tucked away in one of the cycle's storage compartments, she started to walk toward the three of them.

"Neat bike," Michael said.

"Thanks. You must be—"

"Michael."

"Hi, Michael."

Burt swallowed. "I'm Burt. This is Ryan. Wadsworth is out back."

"I hear he had a run-in with some flowers this morning."

Her grin was infectious, and Burt felt a smile tugging at his mouth.

"Cici was real mad," Ryan volunteered excitedly. "But Dad really yelled at Wadsworth and he let go—"

Burt cleared his throat, uneasy. "Sandy, I don't want you to get the impression that I'm some sort of tyrant."

"Not at all. Why don't we go out back so I can meet Wadsworth?"

Ryan led the way, his short legs pumping furiously as he ran toward the backyard. "Wadsworth! Sandy's here!"

Sandy fell into step beside Burt, and he noticed the fact that she was tall enough so he didn't have to contort his neck to look down at her. The top of her head came right to his shoulder.

"I don't usually start training until I've observed the dog for a while. I also want to ask you some questions. I don't charge for the first session, because I'll be explaining how I work, and you might find you want to go with someone else's method."

"No, no." Burt unlocked the gate leading to the backyard and ushered everyone through, then locked it behind him. "I'm sure whatever you do will be fine." He couldn't stop looking at her. And she couldn't be over twenty-five. Feeling like some kind of pervert, Burt glanced away from Sandy, turning his attention to the yard.

It looked awful. With his writing going so badly, he hadn't had much energy for yard work. Compared to Cici's pristine *Better Homes and Gardens* yard, his was a mélange of overgrown grass, weeds and huge holes, the latter courtesy of Wadsworth.

"Wadsworth!" Ryan screamed again, at the top of his lungs. Burt knew his son was excited. They so rarely had adult company lately, so Sandy's mere presence was special.

The sheepdog exploded out the dog door and raced toward them. His attention was immediately focused on Sandy and he raced for her, full tilt. Burt saw what he was about to do seconds before he did it.

"Wadsworth, down!"

But it was futile. The dog leaped at Sandy, punching her chest with his paws, and Burt watched in horror as dog and trainer fell to the weed-infested ground.

He was at her side instantly, furious with the dog and himself. As he reached down to give her his hand, his thoughts raced.

What can she possibly be thinking about us?

As Sandy struggled to evade a warm, sloppy pink tongue, she started to laugh. Masses of dog hair were pressed against her face, then the tongue returned.

Out of the corner of her eye she saw Ryan running around them, then darting in and tugging at Wadsworth's hair, trying to pull the animal off her.

"He likes you!" the little boy said excitedly. At the sound of his voice, Wadsworth turned and jumped on top of Ryan.

Sandy rolled to her side and grabbed the sheepdog by his ruff, then eased the large dog off Ryan.

"Calm down, Wadsworth. That's a good boy."

She petted the sheepdog, all the while watching the animal. No real problem here. Just an exuberant dog needing a lot of exercise and attention. A big puppy, really. Wadsworth's hind end wiggled as he took in the sound of her voice and touch of her hands. She started to scratch his head and he closed his eyes in dog ecstasy.

"Sandy, I'm really sorry."

She glanced over at Burt and immediately sensed he was embarrassed.

"No problem. He's just happy to see us. I think we're going to get along just fine."

"I haven't—we—no one has really trained him. I guess we've kind of let him run wild."

She wondered why he bothered having an animal at all. But she decided not to come to any conclusions before she had all the facts.

"We can start now. A dog can learn at any age. How old is he?"

"Eight months, I think."

"You don't know?" This was a little peculiar. "Did you pick him up at a pound?" She wondered if Burt had even bothered to take the sheepdog to the vet.

He looked uncomfortable. "My wife—my ex-wife—brought Wadsworth over one afternoon. For Ryan. I wasn't home or I—" He glanced at his younger son, and Sandy was suddenly aware both boys were watching him intently.

Quickly, acting on her feelings, she decided to bail him out. "I have several questions to ask you, and I'm in dire need of a bathroom. Could I . . . ?" She let the rest of her question trail off.

The look he gave her was grateful, and she knew he was aware of precisely what she'd done.

"I'll show you," Ryan announced. "C'mon, Sandy."

She took Ryan's grubby hand in hers and allowed him to lead her to the back door.

INSIDE THE BATHROOM, Sandy washed her hands slowly as she thought about what she was up against.

They were nice people. Some of her jobs had resulted in her meeting the weirdest people known to mankind. This household was fairly normal. One father, two small sons. She guessed Michael to be around ten, and Ryan five. Burt looked as if he was in his early thirties.

Wadsworth was a case of massive neglect, but even the sheepdog was beginning to make some sense. If Burt's ex-wife had simply dropped the animal off without consulting him, and the children had become excited and emotionally attached to the puppy, she could understand how he would have felt like a first-class bastard explaining why they couldn't keep it.

And parents did things like that. People were only too human. She could even understand the ex-wife, feeling guilty over the divorce and what had happened to her children. Giving them a wonderful present in the shape of an adoring puppy. And sheepdog puppies were especially adorable.

It was an unusual household, a father and his two boys. Usually the mother received custody of the children. Had Burt been ruthless and demanded that he receive custody?

As she dried her hands on one of the small towels, Sandy rejected that idea immediately. He didn't seem like the sort of man who would get ugly in a fight. But then, divorce sometimes brought out the worst in two people.

There was something... She paused at the door, needing just a few more seconds to collect her thoughts. The same instincts that helped her with dog training were often effortlessly brought into play with people.

She had sensed an air of...of *sadness*. As if all three of them were silently hurting.

She closed her eyes and tried to focus on the picture they had presented. Burt, in worn jeans and a red sweatshirt. His face looked strained and he had slight circles beneath his eyes. He was worried about something.

Michael. Dressed in a black kimono top and black pants, a headband in his straight brown hair. He'd been admiring of her bike and talkative for just an instant, then had fallen silent. She knew the Ninja fashions were all the rage for boys his age in the valley. He probably played such games with his friends. But she felt as if he were holding a lot of emotion inside.

And Ryan. Sandy smiled, remembering the determined little boy dressed in army camouflage pants and a Gumby and Pokey T-shirt. Too loud, too fast, too eager. He was in need of a friend, and was willing to latch on to anyone. She determined to be especially kind to him.

And as Sandy opened her eyes and reached for the doorknob, she wondered what kind of mother gave her youngest child a pet so likely to overwhelm him.

BURT LOOKED UP as Sandy walked into the kitchen.

"Would you like something to drink? It's been so hot this summer. I've got Pepsi, 7-Up, orange juice...." He knew he was babbling, but there was something about her that made him nervous.

"Pepsi'd be fine."

He opened a can and handed it to her, then took one for himself.

"Well," Sandy said, "Wadsworth is going to take a lot of work, but I know he's up to it. Sheepdogs can be pretty stubborn, but they're smart. I think as long as he knows we mean business, we'll be able to handle him."

Burt took a long swallow of his soft drink, then set the can down in front of him. "I know what it must look like, the yard a mess and the dog running wild. This morning, when he went after Cici's flowers, I knew I had to do something. We saw the ad on television, and I thought that training would be easier than getting rid of him. I don't mean that like it sounds—"

"I know what you mean. Sometimes you reach the end of your rope, and you have to think of all your alternatives. And I know how frustrating a dog can be."

She understands. He could feel himself beginning to relax, now that he knew she wasn't going to sit in judgment over him. And he couldn't stop looking at her. She was pretty in such a fresh, unspoiled way. Even sitting in dirt-smeared jeans and a blue sweatshirt covered with dog hair, she was still pretty.

"Well, how does this usually go?" Burt asked, more confident now that things were going to work out. "I suppose you'll set up a time you'll come over every week. I'm here all the time—I work out of the house—so if there's anything you need, I'll be right here."

She stared at him for a moment, then that quick smile spread over her features. He liked the way it reached all the way to her eyes.

But he was surprised by what came out of her mouth.

"Oh, no, Mr. Thomson. I think we have a misunderstanding. I'm here to train Wadsworth, but I also insist on complete participation from any dog's owner."

Chapter Two

Burt turned off the garden hose and surveyed the yard. Much improved. He and the boys had spent one morning filling in all the holes Wadsworth had dug, then filled the last empty one with water. Sandy had been right—Wadsworth hadn't touched it. He'd tried once and had been so surprised when his paws were soaked that he had run to the far corner of the yard. He had crept back after a time and circled it suspiciously, but there had been no more holes dug.

Burt had to admit he'd been inspired after her first visit. Before the holes had been filled in, he had carefully mowed around them and even pulled some of the weeds. Then he and Michael had gathered up the cut grass. Both of his sons had enjoyed working with him, spending time with him. It made Burt feel guilty, that he'd neglected his children. They had been through so much.

In a roundabout way it had even helped John Savage, his fictional character. Though Burt could never envision Savage doing yard work, the sunshine and manual labor had relaxed him, and he'd thought of some solutions to the problems that had been blocking him.

But now he had a distraction of a different sort.

Sandy Hensley. He even liked her name. She had given him her home phone number, and he knew by the area code that she lived over the hill in Los Angeles proper, not in the valley. They had talked at the kitchen table for almost two hours. She had outlined the way they were going to work together, and how she expected him to give Wadsworth a short training session every single day, going over the behavior she had introduced the sheepdog to in that week's lesson.

The only consolation was that he would get to see her every Saturday.

You are ridiculous, thinking about a woman who was Ryan's age when you were in high school. But it was pleasurable, thinking about Sandy. He'd dated several women since the divorce, but not really enjoyed any of them. He was too available, and they were all too obviously marriage minded. After the third date, most of them had subtly—or not so subtly—steered the conversation around toward what they really had in mind. Commitment.

Having been stung once, he was going to be very cautious the second time around. Especially with children. It had taken him so long to convince Michael and Ryan that he wasn't going to disappear from their lives. There had been long nights filled with nightmares and crying from Ryan. Michael had contained so much more of his grief, but he kept a small framed picture of his mother on the table by his bed, and sometimes when Burt passed his half-opened bedroom door and glanced in, he would catch his older son lying in bed and looking at the photo.

Burt was in no hurry. He'd needed the time to regain his emotional equilibrium and get his life in order. His publisher had been most understanding, and had given him double the time it usually took him to finish a book in his John Savage series.

He'd often thought that were he to marry again, the woman involved would have to hit him like a ton of bricks. He still remembered the queer feeling in his chest when Sandy had smiled. He wondered what she was doing, an extremely pretty blonde in Southern California, working with dogs. Her type was usually shooting commercials if not trying out for a television or movie part.

But he liked that aspect of her. She was outdoorsy and uncomplicated. During their kitchen-table talk, she had also outlined a proper diet for Wadsworth, a feeding schedule, and had advised him to take the sheepdog to the vet for a bath and trim.

"You especially have to keep that little bit of hair by his mouth, the part that hangs down, trimmed. It gets wet, or food gets on it, and it can be unhealthy for him."

He had agreed to everything and the same day, after she left, he had phoned and made an appointment with a local vet to take Wadsworth for a bath the following week. Sandy agreed to come on Saturdays so the boys could watch the training sessions. Ryan had a playschool group three days a week, and Michael was taking swimming lessons, but Burt had always kept Saturdays open for family outings. This would be something they could all do together. He felt it would be a useful way for them to learn a sense of responsibility.

What he liked best about Sandy was the uncomplicated way she seemed to accept the choices he had made. He couldn't give Wadsworth away. The darn dog meant too much to Ryan. Michael seemed to be able to take him or leave him—and Burt suspected his older son still held in a great deal of anger toward his mother—but Ryan adored the clumsy sheepdog, and Burt didn't have the heart to hurt him further.

Now, as he walked toward the back door, he glanced back to the large tree where Michael and Ryan were playing up in the tree house he had built for them two summers ago.

"Michael," he called.

"Yeah, Dad?"

"Watch your little brother. I'll be inside taking a shower."

"Okay."

That was unusual. But one could be thankful for small things. At least Michael had decided to be nice to Ryan for a change.

A hot shower sounded better and better. He flexed his sore shoulders and headed inside.

"So what do you think, Sandy? How would you define love?" Elaine placed the plate of spaghetti in front of her, and Sandy suddenly realized that it sounded as if she had asked the question a second time.

"I guess...well, maybe if you're thinking about that person a lot of the time. You mean in the beginning, or the type of love where you think you're ready to get married?''

"I mean in the beginning. Start eating, it's no good when it's cold."

Sandy picked up her fork as she glanced at her two roommates. She had met Elaine Harrison when she'd come to her house to train her Lhasa apso, Lola. The dog had required only three sessions, but she and Elaine had hit it off immediately. Elaine had asked her to house-sit several times, as she was vice president of her father's cosmetic company and was forever jetting off to Europe to see what the latest cosmetics craze was. Their other roommate, Fred Meyer, was a stand-up comic and had met Elaine when she had gone to school at UCSB. He had moved to Los Angeles from New York almost a year ago.

It had been only a matter of time after Lola's obedience training before Elaine asked Sandy to move in and share her house. It was a large stucco mansion, built in the twenties and perched up in the Hollywood Hills. Even with two women living there, they still rattled around. Fred lived out in the guest house by the pool.

Now their household numbered three people, two dogs, a cat and three hamsters.

"In the beginning, I think it's mostly chemistry."

"Have you ever been really bowled over by anyone?" Elaine had her back to her, dishing up Fred's plate while he was struggling to open a bottle of wine. As Sandy began to pick at her dinner, she thought of how lucky she was to have such caring friends for housemates. She'd had a particularly horrendous day, taking Mark's assignment and working with the Corsinos' stubborn bulldog. She'd come home smelling and feeling like garbage.

"Yeah." She couldn't be anything but honest with these two. They'd find out sooner or later. When you lived with anyone for any length of time, they grew sensitive to your moods.

"What happened?"

She took a deep breath. "I just met him last Saturday."

"Whoa." Fred picked up one of the wineglasses and began to pour. "Start from the beginning."

"There isn't much to tell. I was sent out to see to his dog, and when I met him—I don't know, I just felt—"

"Lust."

"Fred." Elaine mock-glared at him as she set his plate on the table. "Must you always reduce something as profound as love to a basic animal urge?"

"It's the truth. It's your glands talking in the beginning, and I have an infallible test for proving I'm right. Sandy, you say you're attracted to this man?"

She nodded, knowing Fred was going to drop a verbal bombshell. He was a funny man. He looked at life with a peculiar twist that was all his own. But what separated him from a lot of other comics was that he never used his humor to hurt, and never reduced his various routines to the easy laughs built around sex, drugs and insult humor.

At home, of course, it was different, and they talked about everything.

"Here's the clincher. Have you thought about what he looks like with his clothes off?"

Elaine rolled her eyes as she sat down, then reached for her glass of wine. "Don't answer that, Sandy. Take the Fifth."

"According to statistics," Sandy began, a hint of mischief in her voice, "the average man thinks about sex and has a sexual thought every six minutes. And I don't think the average woman is far behind. Now, I spent the better part of two and half hours with this man, so therefore—"

"You thought about him sexually twenty-five times in the amount of time you were there," Fred finished for her. "And that doesn't even count what you might have thought as you came home, or in the days since, or what you were thinking about while you were taking your shower upstairs. But what about the clothes? Were they on or off?"

Sandy took a sip of wine, then answered coolly, "Fred, when a woman fantasizes a sexual experience, it's a lot less—"

"Down and dirty," Elaine said.

"Well, it's more . . . romantic."

"Okay, so you had soft lights and music playing. Did the guy have his clothes off? A bare chest? Great legs? Buns?"

"You are disgusting," Elaine teased.

"I ask the questions no one else will ask. C'mon, Sandy, prove my theory correct."

Sandy leaned back in her chair and grinned. "My thoughts about this man have been pretty spectacular," she admitted.

"What does he look like?" Elaine asked.

"Who's that guy who was in that movie—you know, the one that swept the Oscars last year?"

"*Platoon*. Charlie Sheen."

"No way, too young. The one with the scarred face."

"Tom Berenger."

"That's it. He looks like Tom Berenger, but a little older. He has just the tiniest amount of gray in his hair, but his face is really similar. That's about the best I can do."

"Tall?" Elaine quizzed.

"Taller than me."

"Then he's almost six feet," Fred observed.

"Nice body?" Elaine continued.

"He moves like a guy who used to be into sports. And he's kept himself in shape."

"So what's to stop you?" Fred asked. "You lure him out into the yard, unclip the dog's leash, use the leather to tie him up and throw him to the ground and have your wicked way with him."

"That same article said men have much more direct methods of seduction—if you can call it that."

"Okay, okay. So you grab a few candles and spray the sheets with cologne and drag him back into his bedroom. I can guarantee you, the guy will love it."

"He has two children."

Her announcement was greeted with dead silence.

"Divorced, I hope," Elaine said after a moment.

"Yes. His ex gave the littlest boy the dog, and they've kind of let Wadsworth run wild."

"Wadsworth?" Fred asked. "What kind of dog?"

"English sheepdog."

"For a kid? Those are big dogs."

"Big guilt," Elaine said.

"You got it."

"He has the kids?" Fred asked.

"He has custody. This man doesn't strike me as a weekend father."

"It complicates things a little," Fred began. "I mean, seduction is difficult under any circumstances, but with a little ingenuity—"

"I want to get to know him. I don't want to rush anything. He may still be hurting, and I don't want to add to that hurt."

"You really like this guy," Elaine said.

"Yeah. I really do."

"SANDY, I KNOW I'm going to sound like I'm breaking our agreement, but could you work with Wadsworth alone today and show me what to do at the end of the session?" Burt felt miserable having to voice this particular request, but he was desperate.

"What happened?"

Her voice was soft and encouraging; that was a good sign. "Ryan had an infection. I think some water got into his ear. He was really in pain and I couldn't leave him alone. Now I'm running behind schedule. But I did work with Wadsworth every day."

"It's okay. Get going on the book. I'll work with the big guy today."

"You're a doll."

She watched him lope back to the house and in the back door. Then she glanced down at Wadsworth, whose attention had been intently focused on his exiting master.

"No way, buddy. You and I have a lot of work to do."

AFTER THE SESSION, Sandy unhooked Wadsworth's leash and watched, amused, as the shaggy dog bounded into the far end of the yard. He was an intelligent animal. He'd calmed down considerably—probably because of the time Burt was spending with him—and was slightly less rambunctious. She'd been afraid the sheepdog was going to hurt Ryan when he leaped on top of the little boy, so she had taken drastic measures. Every time Wadsworth jumped up on her, she gave him a corrective jerk with the leash and choke collar or lightly stepped on the dog's hind paws. Either method taught a dog not to jump up and possibly hurt someone.

Now she stepped inside the back door and into the kitchen. Sandy quietly hung up Wadsworth's leash and decided she would ask one of the boys to show her where their father's study was. Then she would interrupt Burt long enough to explain what had to be done that week. If he was totally involved with his work, she would leave him a note.

As she walked into the living room, she found Ryan lying on the couch, a worried expression on his face.

"Hey, Ryan. What're you up to?"

"I'm in trouble."

"Oh, no. What happened?"

His eyes filled with tears as he looked up at her. "I have to bring cupcakes."

"Where?"

"To scouts."

"When?"

"Tomorrow."

"That's plenty of time."

"But Daddy will be mad because I waited for the last minute. And he burns them. No one will want to eat them."

"Let's think of a solution. Maybe your dad could buy some at the bakery."

"He's too busy blowing up Russia."

She had to stifle the urge to laugh. "Maybe I can help you. We could go down to the market and pick up a mix."

Ryan's face filled with a desperate hope and she resisted the urge to reach out and hug him. He was so cute, with his round little face and stocky body.

"Now, we need a few things. Do you have a cupcake pan?"

"I think Daddy burned it."

They rummaged through the kitchen until Sandy found one.

"Okay, now we have to leave a note."

"Why? Daddy won't come out until dinner."

"Let's leave him a note. He'll be worried if he doesn't know where you are."

Sandy scribbled a note and tacked it to the refrigerator with a magnet, then she took Ryan's hand and they started out the front door.

They walked all the way down to Ventura Boulevard. It was quite a distance to the nearest market, but she couldn't have perched Ryan on her cycle and she didn't feel she could ask to borrow the car. Besides, exercise was good for little boys. Ryan chattered the entire way, telling her about dinosaur week at his playschool and the picture he was painting for his father.

They reached the market, and soon were pushing a cart down the aisle stocked with baking supplies.

"What do you think, Ryan? I like Duncan Hines myself."

"Chocolate."

Sandy was squatting in the aisle, examining the ingredients list on a box of cake mix when she heard a feminine voice exclaim, "Ryan, what are you doing here without your father? Is Burt in the store?"

Sandy glanced up and saw a slender blonde. Her pale hair was pulled back in a sleek knot. Her turquoise cotton pants and turquoise and white sweater were cool and flattering. Sandy knew at a glance that her sandals, though simple in design, were leather and expensive. Her toenails were painted a pale shade of pink, her nails perfectly manicured.

In vivid contrast, Sandy's jeans were lightly dusted with dog hair, and her khaki, short-sleeved shirt was damp with perspiration. She'd changed from the boots she wore riding her motorcycle to worn Reeboks. One of her laces had a knot in it. She'd thought of impressing Burt with what a great dresser she was, but had decided he couldn't possibly expect her to dress up to train a dog.

"Sandy is going to make me cupcakes!" Ryan announced.

"Really." The cool blonde said this in the same tone one would use upon finding a moldy piece of bread beneath one's bed.

"Chocolate ones!"

"From a mix? Not from scratch?"

Sandy rose slowly, using her height to her advantage. She'd shot up in the eighth grade and despaired of ever finding a dance partner tall enough for her. Now she was comfortable with all five feet eight inches, and she looked down at the top of this woman's perfectly coiffed head.

"Hi, I'm Sandy Hensley. Burt hired me to train Wadsworth." Though all her instincts were screaming against liking this woman, she decided to grit her teeth and give her the benefit of the doubt.

"Cici Forrest. I live next door."

Wadsworth. The flowers.

"Ah. It must have been your garden that was ravaged."

Cici did not look amused. "Yes. So you work for Burt?" This was said a little too brightly.

I get it. Sandy took in the proprietary vibrations this woman was giving off.

"Until Wadsworth learns to behave himself."

"We filled up all the holes," Ryan said. "Cici, can I come over and fill the holes by your house?"

"Maybe another time, Ryan." She turned her attention back to Sandy. "You don't have to trouble yourself, Sandy. I bake all the time. It would be nothing for me to make a few cupcakes."

"No!" Ryan tugged at her shirttail, and Sandy smiled down at the little boy.

"Ah, we don't have anything else to do, do we, Ryan?"

"Nope."

"Well...I see. Ryan, next time you need something, come over and ask me, all right?"

Slowly Ryan nodded his head.

Cici continued up the aisle, stopping only to select a large bag of sugar. She scanned the shelves for another second, then turned her cart and disappeared around the corner of a display.

Sandy quickly picked up a can of frosting, some colored sprinkles and some paper baking cups. Then, hoping against hope they wouldn't run into Stepford Wives Cici Forrest again, she steered Ryan toward the dairy section and picked up a dozen eggs and a small carton of milk.

"Anything else?" she asked Ryan.

"Candy?" he asked hopefully.

"How about gum?"

"Okay."

Within the hour they were back at the house. Sandy measured all the liquids and let Ryan pour them into the cake mix, then she mixed them quickly and poured the batter into the baking cups. Sliding the cupcake tray inside the preheated oven, Sandy closed the door and turned to Ryan.

"That was pretty easy problem solving. Now we have to watch the clock so they won't burn."

"Can we open the frosting and eat some? My friend's mom lets me."

"Hmm. Why don't we get two spoons and lick out the bowl?"

"Yeah!" As Ryan raced for the silverware drawer, Sandy started to laugh.

THE SMELL OF BURNING GUNPOWDER assaulted his nostrils. Savage's eyes were burned by the thick smoke as he fought his way out of the—

Burt stopped typing abruptly. He was almost finished for the day, and it had been quite a productive session. However, at the same time John Savage's nostrils were being assaulted by smoke, his were being teased by the distinctive aroma of baking chocolate.

There was no contest between the two. He saved his work, then exited from the program, removed the discs and shut off his computer.

When he opened the door to the long hallway, the scent was stronger. He followed his nose to the kitchen, and saw Ryan sitting at the table, his mouth ringed with chocolate batter. He was carefully putting sprinkles on top of a perfectly frosted chocolate cupcake.

Sandy was sitting across from him. She was frosting cupcakes with a graceful economy of motion, her knife moving deftly. As soon as Ryan finished sprinkling the cupcake in his possession, she placed it on a cookie sheet and handed him the one she had just finished frosting.

"Daddy!" Ryan caught sight of him, and Burt reached down and ruffled his hair.

"What're you doing here, Ryan?"

"Sandy made me cupcakes."

"Just like that, huh?"

"I asked her."

"I hope it's okay." Now Sandy was looking up at him, her hands stilled. It surprised him to see that she seemed a little nervous. "He said he needed them for scouts tomorrow, and he was worried, so I thought it wouldn't take too much time. We didn't disturb you, did we?"

"Not at all."

"Eat one, Daddy." Ryan held out a cupcake and Burt took it and began to peel off the paper.

"They smell great. Thanks, Sandy. I appreciate it. You saved me a last-minute trip to the bakery."

"It was fun." She pushed back her chair. "I'd better get going. It's getting late."

"I've got a better idea," Burt said, inspiration striking. "The least I can do to repay the favor is have you stay for dinner. We'll order in a pizza and you can tell me what you and Wadsworth did today. Your choice on the pizza."

She was about to refuse and offer an excuse of previous plans, but something in his expression prevented her. He was lonely. The way his face had lit up with the suggestion, the slight eagerness in his eyes. She wondered about his life, about the days he spent alone in his studio and the evenings he spent eating dinner with his sons for company.

He was an excellent father. But everyone needed adult company.

"That would be really nice. Pepperoni and green pepper?"

Ryan made a gagging sound.

"You don't like pepperoni?" she asked him.

He started to laugh.

"Just pepperoni is fine."

Burt smiled at her and turned toward the phone. He consulted a list of numbers written on a magnetic pad, then dialed and ordered the pizza. Sandy busied herself cleaning up the mess from the cupcakes. She showed Ryan where she put them in the cupboard, then wiped down the small kitchen table.

"Sit down, Sandy. You've worked hard enough for today."

"I don't think training a dog and making cupcakes is particularly exhausting."

"I'll make a salad. You relax."

Halfway through the salad, the phone rang. It was Michael, asking if he could stay at a friend's for dinner. Burt gave him permission, and so it was just the three of them for the informal supper.

When Burt returned to the kitchen table and sat down, Sandy decided she wanted to get to know this man better.

"How's the writing going?" she asked.

"Better. Than it has been, I mean."

Ryan was totally absorbed in his pizza. The little boy had seemed happy she was staying, and much more relaxed since he knew his cupcakes were safely up in the cupboard and ready for tomorrow.

"Have you been having trouble?" She liked looking at Burt's eyes. They were so blue. He'd seemed tired when he'd first come into the kitchen and seen them baking cupcakes, but now it was as if he'd come into a reserve of energy. She didn't want to overstay her welcome or impose on Burt and his family, so she had been carefully watching his mood all through dinner.

"I don't really know what it is. It's rare for me to be blocked. When I first started writing, I did it in my spare time, so I couldn't afford the luxury."

"What did you do before you worked at home?"

"Advertising. It was a great training ground."

"A lot of writers seem to come up that way." She leaned back in her chair, her dinner finished, and reached for her glass of milk. "What kind of story are you writing?"

"It's an action-adventure book, part of a series. I created this man, John Savage. He's a James Bond type character, always going into countries and straightening things out. Getting involved with fabulous women, making the world a safer place, that sort of thing."

She liked the way he wasn't self-deprecating, the way he didn't make what he did seem like a joke. She'd met a lot of writers during her dog-training days, and it seemed that so many of them were still waiting for the main chance, whether it was the Great American Novel, Screenplay or Play. Invariably she found those types of writers boring. They were either too wrapped up in themselves or they refused to live in the moment and continued to look hazily off into what they considered a legitimate future.

"It sounds like you like him."

"Most of the time I do. It's just that lately—"

She waited for him to continue.

It didn't take long.

"It's so strange. I'm not usually blocked. I'm not having a good time with this book, and I'm not sure why."

"Sometimes when you have a lot of stress in your life, it's hard to concentrate on other things." She remembered Burt as she had first met him, the fine lines of tension around his eyes and mouth, the pale skin. She wasn't quite sure why she'd jumped in like that, but she had. Now she could only hope she hadn't made him totally uncomfortable.

He hesitated a moment, and she could see his slight apprehension. And she wondered about the woman he had married and what had happened to their relationship.

It was funny the way she thought about people. So much of her thinking was based on what she had learned while training dogs. People needed love and appreciation, and a sense of purpose in their lives. She liked people and found that, most of the time, when she helped a dog live up to his fullest potential his owner wasn't far behind. She was a firm believer in animals bringing out the best in people, and Burt was no exception.

Her heart had gone out to him immediately. It had been clear to her he had had no idea what to do with Wadsworth, but now that the sheepdog was in the process of being trained, the end to all this confusion was in sight.

Burt glanced at Ryan, busily eating his pizza and dripping a generous amount of tomato sauce down the front of his Porky Pig T-shirt. Then he returned his attention to her.

"I didn't want to admit it at first. Being stressed, I mean. I thought I should be able to take it."

She shook her head gently and waited for him to continue.

He hesitated for an instant, then the words seemed to tumble out of his mouth. "Men don't let things get to them. At least the men I write about. The men I grew up with." He took a deep breath. "The man I was supposed to be."

She felt a little catch at her heart. He looked so unconsciously vulnerable. She knew he was tired, and that had to be the reason these words were being spoken.

"I think you're being too hard on yourself." She set her glass down, then leaned forward in her chair, her eyes intent on his. She'd come to believe there was no such thing as a perfect, safe moment when one decided to become involved with another person. You just had to jump right in. Fred's opinions to the contrary, she did feel something special for this man. She wasn't going to rush it, but just let things develop slowly.

"You're probably right." Now he seemed a little embarrassed, as if by revealing a part of himself he had made a mistake.

"You look a lot less tense, though." At his look of curiosity, she explained herself. "When I first met you, you seemed kind of harried. I just assumed you were going through a tough time with your writing. But I think being outside and working with Wadsworth has been good for you."

He grinned. "Yeah. It's nice, being out there with him and not wondering about a million other things. Just me and Wadsworth."

At the sound of his name, the sheepdog lazily perked up his ears, then raised his head. He was lying to the side of the kitchen table, and Sandy had seen the soulful eyes look upward, hoping against hope that a piece of pizza would come his way.

She sensed that Burt was slightly embarrassed, and steered the conversation into safer ground. They talked about Wadsworth's next lesson, how the sheepdog was progressing, what he had done that afternoon.

Then, very deliberately, she brought up the subject of Cici Forrest.

"I met your neighbor at the market."

"Cici?"

"Uh-huh. She offered to bake cupcakes for Ryan, but I was kind of into it at that point." Sandy took a deep breath. "She seems like a nice woman."

"She is. She's had a tough time. She's been married three times, and each husband died. Rotten luck. She went to school with Anne at Vassar, and when she moved out here after the death of her second husband, the house next door to us was up for sale. Anne convinced her to buy it."

"She must be quite a gardener."

"She is. I replaced those lilies. You know, I never knew flowers could be so expensive."

Sandy watched Burt's face carefully throughout the discussion, and never saw a hint of knowledge concerning what Cici really had in mind. Men could be so dense at times. Burt obviously had no idea that Cici's concept of friendship to his ex-wife did not exclude cozying up to the ex-husband.

After dinner, Ryan went into the den to watch a television show and Burt walked Sandy out to her cycle. He stood in the driveway while she changed her sneakers to boots then pulled on her jacket and gloves.

The sky was tinged with color as dusk fell, and the summer air was warm and fragrant with the scent of orange blossoms. Stars were beginning to shimmer in the evening sky.

"I had a great time, Burt. Thanks for asking me to dinner."

He was standing next to her in the driveway. Her back was to her bike, and she was looking up at him.

It seemed he was searching for something in her expression. Or maybe she was just imagining it.

"I really appreciate what you did today, Sandy. Letting me off with Wadsworth and leaving me free to work. And Ryan's cupcakes—he was happy tonight in a way I haven't seen him in a while." He ran his fingers through his hair, and she sensed the next words weren't easy ones, but she knew they were words she wanted to hear.

"It hasn't been easy for him, with his mother gone. I try to do a lot of things with both of them, but it's different."

"Ryan told me you burn cupcakes," she said, wanting to ease his tension with a touch of humor.

"I don't mean it in a sexist way. You know, women bake and men go to work. But there's something different for him when a woman is around. Do you know what I mean?"

"Yes, I do. And I want you to know something, Burt. I hope you don't think I'm trying to butt into your life. I just wanted to help Ryan."

"I know."

"I would never do anything to hurt your children." She looked down, suddenly embarrassed by her outburst.

She felt his hand touch her chin, then gently raise her head so she was looking into his eyes. "I know, Sandy, and I appreciate your being honest with me."

"Okay."

For a long moment he didn't remove his hand, then he slowly released her chin. She resisted the urge to touch her skin, to feel the slight tingle his fingers had produced.

He stepped back and she started to put on her helmet. Before she covered her head, his voice floated out over the warm summer air.

"Next Saturday, if it's as hot as today, bring your suit and we'll swim afterward."

She paused, helmet in one hand, then gave him the thumbs-up signal and smiled.

LATE THAT NIGHT, with both boys in bed, Burt returned to his study and turned on the computer. He worked for two hours and was surprised to find that he actually got some writing done. And it was good; the scene worked.

Afterward he saved the material and exited from the program, then leaned back in his chair and closed his eyes.

He liked Sandy. Really liked her. He'd felt relaxed talking with her across the kitchen table. There had been so many dinners with so many women in fancy restaurants. These women had asked him about his work, how he felt, what he wanted. Yet he had never sensed such absolute caring and warmth as he had from Sandy, sitting across the kitchen table.

She had a way of getting underneath a man's skin.

She was honest. Direct. She hadn't pulled any punches. It was as if she didn't have time for games, and that was fine with him. He had long ago become frustrated with so many of the women he had met since his divorce.

And if he was honest, even Anne hadn't cared about what it was he wanted to do. From the beginning she hadn't understood his need to write, had only cared that he went to work each morning and managed to support the family. During the last years of his marriage, he had never felt at home in the house. Anne had decorated with a flurry of activity, and each time he entered the front door to find a new piece of furniture or a different color on the walls, he'd felt more and more a stranger.

When she had left, the first thing he'd done was change one of the smaller rooms into a writing studio. He'd changed so much of the ranch-style house, in an attempt to erase his marriage from his mind.

And he had become something of a loner, except for a few close friends and his children.

When he had started dating again, it had been so hard. Awkward. Nerve-racking. It was so strange, to be going out with women at the age of thirty-six. He had thought his marriage meant forever.

Then he had settled into a protective phase and talked himself into believing he would never need anyone again. "Anyone" specifically being a woman.

Sitting across the table from Sandy and talking with her had shown him how utterly stupid that thinking was.

It had felt so good talking to a caring adult again.

Be honest with yourself. If talking with a caring adult was all you needed, you could pick up the phone and call Alice. George and Alice, his neighbors four houses down, had been absolute rocks throughout the divorce. He was particularly close to Alice. When he'd become a house husband, she'd always been there for him, willing to help and share her considerable child-raising skills. The two families had been close, as they had children the same age and many of the same joys and problems.

No, there was something else in what he had felt for Sandy. He was attracted to her, had been from the start. He knew she was considerably younger than he was, but he felt so comfortable with her, so close. And it was ridiculous, because he had only known her such a short time.

She just had a way about her.

The invitation to stay after the next lesson and swim had caught him by surprise. He hadn't stopped to think whether it was a smart thing to do or not. He had simply wanted to spend more time with her. He could envision her clearly now, standing next to her bike, giving him the casual thumbs-up gesture.

Her skin had felt warm and smooth when he'd touched her chin. He'd wanted to touch her hair. It had looked so soft in the dusky evening air.

At that moment he'd realized he wanted—needed—to feel close to someone again.

Not someone. Sandy.

He hadn't felt excited by life in such a long time. Months had gone by in which he had concentrated on emotional survival, his and the boys'. Now a woman with shimmering hair, steady gray-blue eyes and a totally spontaneous smile had burst into his life and turned it upside down.

For the longest time he'd felt he'd had walls built up around his heart. He'd been determined no one was ever going to get close enough to hurt him again. Anne had done such a thorough job, and he was sure he had hurt her just as much.

Sandy. He thought of her and smiled. She'd started to scale those walls when he hadn't been looking. And in the end, all that mattered was that he felt happy when he was with her. He wouldn't rush things. He would try to be patient and give this relationship a chance to develop.

He would try to survive until next Saturday.

Chapter Three

"He wouldn't have asked you if he didn't like you. What suit are you going to wear?" Elaine's brown eyes were bloodshot and her auburn hair fell limply around her shoulders. She had just come back from a quick trip to Germany to see about getting a special shipment of eye pencils. Now she sat perched on the edge of Sandy's bed, sipping a cup of strong coffee.

"The turquoise one."

Her roommate's face fell. "That's no better than a racing suit! Sandy, Sandy, if you want this man, you're going to have to use a little imagination!"

"But I don't want to come on too strong. I mean, his two boys will be there."

"Trust me, at five and ten they won't even notice. But Burt will. I think Fred is right. You can never be too subtle with a man." She took another sip of coffee as she contemplated the problem.

"Maybe he asked me because he likes having another adult to talk to," Sandy suggested. "I mean, he might not even be attracted to me."

"I'm suggesting you *create* that attraction. Why don't you wear that black suit I brought you back from Italy? The one that makes you look like something out of *Sports Illustrated.*"

"I'm going with the turquoise. I want to be comfortable and able to swim, not be worried every minute about how I look."

Elaine gave her a wryly disgusted look. "You win. But take something sexy as a cover-up."

WADSWORTH TROTTED OBEDIENTLY after Burt, and Sandy watched in undisguised delight. The sheepdog was comfortable on a leash. He wasn't heeling like a pro yet, but he understood "sit" and this afternoon they had moved on to "stay." The most important aspect of the training was that most of Wadsworth's destructive behavior had stopped. He no longer dug holes. Burt had helped Cici put up temporary stakes around her flower beds, so Wadsworth couldn't reach them. And he had an assortment of rawhide toys he was chewing instead of the sofa.

In Sandy's opinion, much of the destruction had stopped because Wadsworth had become more secure with Burt. She looked on her job as a training experience for the human half of the team as well.

Burt walked Wadsworth over beside her, then told him to sit. The dog obeyed, and Burt was lavish with praise. Then he glanced at Sandy.

"He's terrific," she said. "So are you. That'll do it for today."

Burt unsnapped the leash, and Wadsworth bounded to the farthest end of the large yard and stationed himself beneath the grapefruit tree that held the boys' tree house. He lay down in the cool, shaded earth and rolled onto his back, waving his paws in the air.

"He looks like I feel," Burt admitted, wiping his brow with his upper arm. "Did you bring your suit?"

"It's inside."

"Why don't we swim for a while, then I'll barbecue hamburgers for dinner." He smiled. "I can't cook macaroni and cheese on the grill, and the boys are sick of pizza, so their third choice is always hamburgers. It isn't exactly nouvelle cuisine."

"Nouvelle cuisine leaves me hungry."

He laughed. Burt looked better than the first day she had seen him, pale and stressed. Now, thanks to his daily sessions outside with Wadsworth, he had a slight tan. The tension around his eyes and mouth had lessened. Sandy was a firm believer in sunshine and exercise being an excellent safeguard against stress and depression, and she was glad to see that Wadsworth's training program seemed to be working for Burt.

"I'll get my suit and meet you out by the pool."

Within minutes, inside the small bathroom off the kitchen, Sandy was staring in horror at the small scrap of black bathing suit. She reached into the tote bag again, hoping against hope to see a flash of turquoise, but instead pulled out a large square of brilliant fuchsia-and-black hand-dyed material, and tiny little sandals.

Elaine. Her roommate must have switched suits while she was taking her shower. Her worst fears were confirmed when her fingers closed around a piece of paper. She pulled it out of the bag and quickly unfolded it. "Sandy, don't be mad at me. I only want what's best for you and Burt."

She tore the paper into tiny pieces and flushed it down the toilet, then stared at the tiny bathing suit as if it might come to life.

It was revealing. Though it was a one-piece, the legs were cut almost to her waist and the neckline plunged deeply, held together by a small silver link. There was no back to speak of. It looked like a bikini bottom when you didn't see the front.

There was nothing she could do. She couldn't very well go out fully dressed and tell Burt she had changed her mind. But this was going to look like a blatant attempt at seduction.

The only possible alternative was to try and carry it off, act as if she wore clothing like this all the time and it was no big deal.

She quickly stripped off her jeans, T-shirt and underwear and folded them, placing her clothing in the empty tote bag. Then she stepped into the suit, pulled it on and adjusted it.

At least she wasn't fat. All the exercise she received training dogs, plus her morning runs and three times a week at the gym assured her that her body was trim and toned. Her body was strong, but she didn't look too muscular.

Glancing with dismay at the high-cut legs, Sandy reached for the cover-up and tied it sarong-fashion so it covered as much as possible. Then she slipped on the sandals. She brushed back her hair, applied an extra squeeze of sunscreen to the tip of her nose and her cheekbones and studied herself in the mirror.

She was as ready as she'd ever be.

BURT WAS TREADING WATER in the deep end of the pool, waiting for Ryan to jump off the diving board, when he heard the kitchen door slam shut.

"Sandy!" Ryan called. "Come watch me dive!"

"You don't dive, Ryan. You just jump in." Michael had swum to the shallow end, and now he stood up and slicked his longish hair back from his eyes.

"I do so! It's a cannonball dive, like Daddy said!"

Burt gave Michael his best don't-start-anything look, then glanced over to where Sandy was making her way toward the pool. She looked like something off a South Sea island, the light material of her cover-up whipping against her in the breeze, her long hair floating down her back.

"I want to wait for Sandy to get in the pool," Ryan announced. "Then I'll dive."

"Okay." Burt turned his attention to Sandy and watched her slip off her sandals. There was something supremely graceful, even seductive, in the simple movement, but he was positive she hadn't meant it that way. He liked to watch the way she moved. She had a natural confidence in her body that probably came from all the physical work she did.

Her fingers reached for the knotted material at her breasts, then she slowly unwrapped the length of material and Burt felt his entire mouth go dry.

She was stunning. The baggy, comfortable clothes she'd worn had done nothing to prepare him for the body that had been hidden beneath. Firm, feminine muscle, full breasts, a slender waist and long, long legs.

She didn't display her body, didn't even seem to be aware of the feminine power she possessed. She simply walked to the edge of the pool, by the deep end, and dived in.

He watched as she surfaced, her face tilted up toward the sun so her long strawberry-blond hair was slicked sharply back from her face. Then she looked at him with those clear gray-blue eyes, her lashes spiky and beaded with water, and Burt felt his breath catch in his throat.

He had never seen anything so purely sensual and beautiful.

She stared at him for a moment, as if sensing his mood. He couldn't look away, though he was aware his most personal thoughts were probably written all over his face.

"Watch me!" Ryan called, effectively breaking the moment.

Burt was grateful for the distraction. "Okay, we're all watching."

Then he concentrated on Ryan catapulting himself off the diving board and splashing into the water feet first. Burt watched his son carefully as he kicked furiously to the surface, then paddled over toward him. Ryan grabbed his arms and smiled up at him.

"Did I look like a cannonball?"

"Yep."

"Now I'm going to swim to Sandy."

Burt watched his son, knowing it was ridiculous to envy a five-year-old. But he did. Ryan paddled over to Sandy and she supported him in the deep water.

"That was some dive, Ryan."

"I'm going to do it again."

"Not right away," Burt said.

They swam for a time, then Burt watched as Sandy walked up the steps at the shallow end of the pool and headed toward one of the chaise lounges. She lay down and closed her eyes.

He forced himself to look away and concentrate on anything else, but he couldn't help wondering what she was thinking.

Sandy lay very still, letting the sunshine bathe her face. Her heartbeat was slowing, the fine trembling in her arms and legs was lessening.

Burt had an extremely expressive face. And Elaine had been right. The suit had pulled a response right out of him. She had seen it in his eyes, seconds before Ryan had made his dive. There had been a purely masculine intensity to his gaze, and she had found she couldn't have looked away if she'd wanted to.

Now she was faced with the prospect of spending the rest of the afternoon and early evening with this man, knowing their comfortable camaraderie had shifted and changed into something deeper and more compelling. The first stirrings of awareness had surfaced. It was as if she had seen him for the first time.

Fred's theory aside, she had wondered what Burt looked like with his clothes off. Seeing his bare chest, she wasn't disappointed. His shoulders were broad, he had a good amount of chest hair and there was a distinct muscle definition. She knew, without his getting out of the pool, that his legs would be long and well-muscled, and he wouldn't carry an ounce of extra flesh around his waistline.

He was simply a beautiful male animal.

She wondered why his wife had left him, then decided not to pursue that thought now. The sounds of the boys laughing and shouting could be heard quite clearly, but she kept her eyes shut as she thought.

It wasn't as if she were some frightened virgin. At twenty-six, she wasn't a total stranger to the opposite sex. Growing up with two brothers gave her an added sense of comfort around men.

But there was a part of her that wished they could have eased into this new attraction a little more slowly. And she wondered if her other sessions with Wadsworth were going to be awkward, with this newfound awareness between them.

The front of her bathing suit was almost dry, the June sunshine strong and hot. She flipped over onto her stomach and cradled her face in her arms.

She was half asleep when she felt droplets of cold water on her legs.

Glancing up, she saw Ryan standing at the foot of the chaise.

"Are you tired?"

"No. I'm just drying off."

"Are you going to come back into the pool?"

"In a little bit."

"Do you like me?"

The question tore at her heart.

"Yes, I do. Very much."

"Do you like Michael?"

She thought of Burt's older son. He hadn't participated much with Wadsworth's training, even though both boys attended the training sessions. He seemed to prefer to be out of the house for long periods of time with his friends, or else he spent time alone in his room. She couldn't really say she felt she knew him at all.

"Yes."

"Do you like my daddy?" There was nothing but the purest innocence in his eyes.

"Yes."

"Can I sit in your chair with you?"

"Sure."

She rolled over onto her back and Ryan clambered up next to her. His body felt cold and wet next to hers, but she clenched her teeth and refused the urge to pull away. Ryan needed affection. In a crazy kind of way, he reminded her of a tiny Wadsworth.

"Where's your house?" Ryan asked, and Sandy sensed she was in for a barrage of questions.

"In Hollywood."

"Can I come visit you?"

"If your dad says it's all right."

"Daddy, can I go to Sandy's house?"

Startled, she looked up to see Burt walking toward them.

"Only if she invites you." His grin was amused, and Sandy sat up slightly on her lounge, grateful that their intense awareness of each other had been shifted aside for the moment.

"She did. Can I go?"

"We'll see."

"Do you have a dog?" Ryan was off and running with his questions again.

"I have a black dog named Panda."

"Like Panda Bear?"

"Uh-huh."

"Does she dig holes like Wadsworth?"

"No."

"Does she sleep on your bed?"

"She sleeps on the floor by my bed."

"Do you have a cat?"

"No. My roommate Fred has a cat." She was aware of Burt's scrutiny as he lay on the lounge next to them. Michael had also left the pool, but he was seated in a chaise slightly away from them, his cassette player was in the shade on one of the tables. He seemed somehow isolated from the three of them, intently listening to his music.

"Is that all your pets?"

She smiled down at the little boy looking up at her so earnestly, then gave in to an impulse and ruffled his wet hair until it stood up in spikes. Ryan laughed, but he didn't pull away.

"I have a baby hamster."

"You have a hamster? We have one at school. His name is Butch and we feed him carrots."

Ryan continued to talk excitedly about Butch, and Sandy looked up slowly, knowing Burt was watching her.

But it wasn't a look that stripped her naked, or conveyed how aware he was of her as a female. His blue eyes were warm, filled with enjoyment. Sandy caught her breath as she realized nothing had been spoiled. It was simply a new beginning.

Ryan told them how Butch ran on a wheel, how he slept during most of the day but sometimes came out of his nest, and how each morning a different classmate got to clean out his bowl and put seeds into it.

"Does Butch have an exercise ball?" Sandy asked.

When it was clear Ryan didn't know what she was talking about, she told him about her own hamster and how in the evenings she put the small animal in a plastic ball and let him run all over the room.

"They like to explore."

"Poor Butch. He just has to sit in his cage."

"Maybe we can buy Butch an exercise ball and take it to your teacher," Burt suggested.

"Okay. I'll tell her tomorrow. Now I'm going to dive." And Ryan jumped up and began to run toward the board.

"Ryan! Not unless I'm in the pool."

"Then jump in!"

"Give me time." Burt stood and stretched slightly. He turned to Sandy. "I haven't spent an afternoon by the pool in a long time. It feels good."

"Thank you for asking me."

"My pleasure."

"Sandy!" Ryan was clambering up on the diving board. "I want you to dive off first."

Her suit was completely dry, her skin warmed by the sun. The only way she could possibly return to the cool water was by jumping in.

"Okay. But you have to get down, Ryan."

Burt was walking down the steps in the shallow end, but he paused to watch Sandy approach the board, enjoying the gentle sway of her hips. It was an extremely pleasurable sight.

She climbed up on the board, curling her bare toes against the rough surface. Burt was in the water now, at the shallow end, and she looked down at him and decided to shake him up. She'd been part of the diving team in high school, and could still do some of the more simple dives.

"Don't fall on me," he called, a teasing glint in his eyes.

She liked this side of him.

"Not a chance."

She loved the simple, clean moves of diving. Balancing herself on the board, she quickly visualized the dive, then stepped forward and bounced high into the air. It was a simple dive, tucking her arms quickly around her knees as she flipped, then arching her body and slicing into the water. She opened her eyes when she touched the bottom of the pool, feeling ridiculously proud of herself. She could see Burt standing in the water toward the shallow end, and she swam vigorously toward him.

She'd meant to surface next to him just to startle him, but she misjudged the distance. As she came out of the water, her body bumped against his and she fell against his bare chest, her hands grasping his shoulders in a futile attempt to steady herself. His hands shot out and clasped her upper arms to steady her. The tips of her breasts brushed his chest, and for one agonizingly long moment they simply stared at each other.

Sandy was intensely aware of him, of the warmth and hard muscles of his body, the shock in his blue eyes quickly replaced by awareness. Regaining her footing on the bottom of the pool, she moved back, her hands leaving his warm, smooth skin. But she couldn't look away. Her mouth felt dry, and she swallowed to ease the sudden tightness in her throat.

It seemed like a long time as they studied each other, but it couldn't have been more than a few seconds. Then Sandy looked away, and her gaze collided with

Michael's. The boy was watching her, awareness in his blue eyes, and Sandy knew that though he might not be completely aware of what had just transpired, his instincts were making up for the gaps in his knowledge.

She didn't even attempt a reassuring smile, knowing only that, to Burt's older son, she was not welcome in the Thomson home.

IT WAS LATE AFTERNOON by the time they finally ate. Sandy had brought a fruit salad and some banana bread—this time from scratch, from Elaine's recipe. Burt tended to the hamburgers and made a pasta and vegetable salad. Michael silently set the table. He wasn't openly hostile, but to Sandy it was easy to see he wasn't happy with her presence. Ryan darted around all three of them, trying to help and generally getting in the way. But no one really minded.

Afterward Burt brought out a carton of strawberry ice cream and a package of sugar cones. They sat around the redwood picnic table, savoring the cool sweetness of the dessert.

Sandy had covertly watched Michael throughout the meal. His emotions were much more guarded than either his brother's or his father's. He kept his eyes lowered much of the time, because their expression was a complete giveaway to his emotional state. They were a lighter blue than either Burt's or Ryan's, and his hair was lighter and straighter. Sandy had realized while studying him that he had to resemble his mother.

He excused himself from the table soon after the meal was finished, claiming there was something on television he wanted to see. Ryan was perfectly content where he was, making a total mess of his ice cream and asking Sandy to tell him stories about her hamster, Camille.

She obliged him, and when she ran out of factual stories she made up a few. She felt comfortable with Burt and his younger son, but there was a nagging sense of guilt underlying everything. If it hadn't been for her, Michael would still be at the table, enjoying time with his father.

Sandy was about to make her excuses and leave when a familiar voice floated out into the evening air.

"Hello, Burt. I meant to drop these by earlier, but it was so hot out that I— Oh, I didn't know you had company."

Cici, looking cool and collected in a pastel pink cotton sundress, stepped around the corner of the house. She was carrying a basket covered with a white cloth, and her hair was pulled back in its usual sleek chignon. Sandy suddenly remembered that when she had changed back into her T-shirt and jeans, her nose had been sunburned. She had combed out her hair and quickly braided it down her back. Casual and elegant she wasn't.

"Come on over, Cici." Burt seemed relaxed around the woman, and Sandy marveled once again at how men could be so oblivious of certain feminine behavior.

Wadsworth, lying beneath the picnic table, began to stir, and Cici gave the dog a nervous glance.

"Burt, Wadsworth isn't going to—"

As much as she would have liked to see the sheep-dog's pawprints all over the bodice of Cici's dress, Sandy slipped several fingers beneath Wadsworth's rolled leather collar. "You stay, Wadsworth." When the dog relaxed against the concrete again, she let go.

"Do you want some ice cream?" Ryan asked.

"No, thank you. I just came by to drop off these muffins. I was baking today, and it was no trouble at all to double the recipe."

Sandy determined to be gracious if it killed her. "They look fabulous. What kind are they?"

"California orange and carrot. They were on the cover of *Good Housekeeping* this month. You might try the recipe, Cindy." A look of consternation crossed her cool, patrician features. "Oh, but I forgot. You don't make things from scratch."

Sandy resisted the urge to kick Cici's elegantly sandaled foot. Instead she smiled, while simultaneously biting her tongue.

"Sandy did a great job with this banana bread," Burt said. "You two might switch recipes."

"Betty Crocker in a box?" Cici asked. "I've never been able to understand using a mix when it takes just a few more minutes to make it from scratch."

"I had some time last night, so I made it from scratch." Sandy hated to turn the conversation so deliberately to her dubious achievement, but she'd be damned if she'd let Cici make her feel incompetent.

"Really?" Cici's eyes widened.

"It's very good," Burt said.

"Cici," Ryan piped up, scuffing the concrete with his sneaker, "when can I come over and fill up the holes Wadsworth dug?"

Sandy stifled a laugh as she watched Cici's facial expression. The woman obviously didn't care for the mess a small child would make in her yard. "I don't know, Ryan. You'll have to ask your father." And she looked over at Burt with eyes that clearly told him how all-powerful she thought he was.

I'm going to throw up. Sandy decided to explain Cici to Elaine and see what her friend could come up with in the way of retaliatory tactics. Perhaps she could break into her house and stock her shelves with packaged cake and muffin mixes. Cici would probably have a coronary.

"We'll see, Ryan. We don't want to do too much yard work, not with this heat."

"We could fill all the holes with water. That would be fun." His eyes were hopeful.

Sandy had to bite her tongue firmly when she saw the aghast look on Cici's face. But she quickly recovered her composure, then said, "I just wanted to drop these muffins off, Burt. You know, I worry about you not eating properly. And working so hard on that book. How is it coming along?"

As Burt replied, Sandy thought of the competent way he had grilled the hamburgers, the quick salad he had tossed together. No one in the Thomson family was in danger of starving. Cici's act was like something out of a fifties sitcom. Only it wasn't as funny.

When Burt finished discussing his book-in-progress with Cici, he glanced down at Ryan. The five-year-old was covered with equal amounts of dirt and dog hair, with smatterings of melted ice cream spread over his Bugs Bunny T-shirt. "I think you'd better take a bath before you go to bed."

Sandy stood up, hoping Cici would take the hint and leave. "I'll clear off the table, Burt."

"Nonsense." Now Cici was all efficiency and perkiness. "You still have to drive a long way home, while I can just walk across the yard. I'll clear up."

The better to get me out of here.

Then Burt surprised her. "I'll walk you outside."

Sandy had the pleasure of seeing Cici's carefully glossed lips tighten just a fraction before she began to busy herself gathering up the paper plates.

"Goodbye, Sandy. Will you come back tomorrow?" Ryan asked. "We could swim in the pool again."

"Oh, honey, I have two dogs to train. But I'll see you next Saturday."

He thought about this for a minute, then said, "Okay. Daddy, can I watch television with Michael just a little bit?"

"Just a little bit."

Sandy's heart speeded up a fraction as she realized she and Burt would be alone outside. With Cici occupied and both boys in the den with the television, she would have him to herself for a few minutes.

As she gathered her tote bag from the bathroom, she glanced at her face in the mirror and saw her cheeks were flushed. What did she expect Burt to do? She made sure all her belongings were in her bag, then as she walked out of the bathroom she decided she would let him set whatever pace he wanted to.

Yet when they both stepped outside, she could feel the tension between them, as palpable as it had been when she had held on to his shoulders for support.

They walked toward her cycle and he stood beside her in the driveway as she pulled on her boots and stowed her sneakers and canvas tote bag in the storage compartment. She was about to pull on her jacket and gloves, but then thought how intimidating all that clothing would be. Elaine had switched swimsuits for a reason. Sandy had seen the expression in Burt's eyes. Now she wanted to give him every possible chance to let their relationship develop.

The swiftness with which it was progressing no longer worried her, as long as they could still remain friendly. As long as adding a sexual element didn't turn Burt into some sort of macho machine and she never got a glimpse of the man she had really liked in the beginning.

She turned to face him, her hands feeling awkward at her sides. Her tongue felt too big for her mouth, and she clenched her fingers into fists to keep from leaning into him. She knew how she felt. Now she wanted to see what moves he would make.

She couldn't see his face, but she could feel the tension in him. For just a moment, she wondered why she had hesitated to don her jacket, what she had thought could happen if she delayed the moment. She even imagined she had mistaken the look in his eyes when they were in the pool.

"How do you feel about spontaneity?" he asked softly. "Does it frighten you to have people act on their feelings?"

She knew what he was asking her, but the words were so exciting she could only shake her head.

"Good," he said softly. He moved quickly, just two steps, then both his large hands were cupping her face as he lowered his mouth to hers.

His kiss was assured, hot and compelling. She met his action with her own, her arms going around his back for support, her body arching softly against his. She knew he felt her response, heard the soft masculine sound of pleasure as his lips left hers for a second then touched hers again in another kiss, moving, tasting, caressing. Her fingers dug into his back as she felt one of his hands move, sliding into her hair, while the other began to slowly caress her back.

Almost a minute later she broke the kiss, taking in deep breaths of the soft, summer air as if she had been running a great distance. She leaned her forehead against his; they were almost the same height with her boots on and him barefoot.

"Oh." It was a woefully inadequate sound, but all she could think of. Her mind was a complete blank, her body alive and humming with exquisite tension.

"It was that swimsuit," he said softly. "You really got to me."

She laughed shakily, delighted she'd gotten under his skin. "I'm glad."

He kissed the side of her mouth softly. "I've got to go back inside."

"I know."

"Be careful going home, okay?"

"I will."

He kissed her one last time, a swift goodbye, then stood back and watched as she put on her jacket and gloves. Sandy fumbled with the zipper, the knowledge that he was watching her making her clumsy. Where did they go from here? Did she just come around every Saturday as planned and give Wadsworth his lesson, or was something more going to happen? Knowing she couldn't endure waiting the week to find out, she took a deep breath and plunged in.

"Speaking of spontaneity..."

"Yes?"

"I'll give you a call."

Her eyes were accustomed to the darkness by now, and she could see his grin. "I'll hold you to that."

"You'll hear from me." She wheeled her motorcycle so it was facing down the drive. He was walking backward toward the house, his eyes still on her.

She lifted her gloved hand in farewell, then started her motorcycle and started down the drive.

Before she turned left at the bottom of the drive, she glanced back.

He was still watching her.

Chapter Four

As Burt lay in bed that evening, he tried to figure out what had come over him and why he had given Sandy that sudden kiss. It wasn't like him.

That wasn't exactly true. It wasn't like what he'd become.

The house was quiet, Wadsworth asleep in the kitchen. The sheepdog liked the cool tile on warm summer nights. Michael and Ryan were asleep in their rooms; he'd checked them a short time ago. There were moments he still couldn't believe Anne had let him have custody. The relationship he had with his sons had deepened over the year and a half they had lived without Anne, and now he couldn't imagine life without them.

He set the magazine he'd been trying to read down on the night table and thought about the kiss. It had been so long since he'd acted on his feelings. After the divorce, he had felt shell shocked. Some days even walking to the end of the driveway to collect the mail had been a major effort. But he had kept up with life, day by day, knowing that if Michael and Ryan saw him crumble it would mean the end of any small feelings of security they had. He had allowed himself to be exhausted and afraid only in the privacy of his own bedroom.

Not that he hadn't shown his sons his pain. Right after the divorce, he had called a friend of his, Jerry Caldwell, a therapist he had met while researching one of his characters. He had gone in for a few sessions, and Jerry had gotten him to talk endlessly of what he was feeling, how overwhelming and confusing life had become. Jerry had convinced him to share selective emotions with his children, and he had had many talks with both boys. But he hadn't felt he had the right to further chip away at the secure foundation he wanted to provide for them.

It was good for them to know Dad didn't have all the answers, and that grown-ups got confused and depressed. But he had never wanted to make them feel he was overwhelmed by them, that he didn't want them with him.

He hadn't been lonely the first year. There was too much pain, and he was simply too busy. For a short time he'd decided he was through with women altogether and would never want to marry again. Then, tentatively, six months ago, he'd started dating. And hated it.

But Sandy . . . He stretched out in bed and put his hands behind his head. She'd attracted him from the start. He could still remember how he'd felt when she'd taken off her helmet and that long blond hair had cascaded down her back. Her face and—especially since the swimsuit—her figure appealed to him, but it went deeper.

She put him at ease. It sounded contradictory because her physical presence heightened his awareness and seemed to charge the very air. But she was also understanding and so...easy. Easy to be with. Uncomplicated.

What he felt for her was anything but.

That kiss. Burt of a cautious nature. Burt, who believed marriage should not even enter a discussion between two consenting adults until they had been seeing each other for a number of months. Burt, who was scared to death of making another emotional mistake.

The words had tumbled out of his mouth and action had followed. He had wanted to kiss her badly. When he'd stepped back from that kiss, he knew he had crossed a significant barrier.

She'd said she would call and he believed her. Sandy wasn't a woman to make false promises.

He was thinking about her, wondering when she would call, when the phone rang.

He picked it up, his heartbeat quickening, wondering if it was...

"Burt?"

He recognized Anne's soft voice instantly.

"Hello, Anne." He settled back against his pillows willing his voice to remain calm. Neutral. His ex-wife had put him through more pain than any other person on earth, but he had determined—with Jerry's professional help—that he was not going to alienate her from the boys, or add to the confusion and messiness of their divorce with behavior that was reprehensible.

He had even congratulated her on her marriage six weeks ago, although he had been extremely relieved that Anne and her new husband had eloped, saving him and the boys from having to make an emotionally uncomfortable appearance.

"Burt, I... I'm not even sure why I feel I have to tell you. It's just that—well, we were together for so long and I do think of you as one of the people I'm closest to. Burt, I . . . I'm pregnant."

Nothing Anne had ever told him, short of the fact that she was leaving to find herself, had ever stunned him this much. He could feel his throat closing. He tilted his head back against the wall and closed his eyes as a peculiar kind of pain washed through him. To be quickly replaced with rage.

"Burt? Are you there?"

"Yes." He forced himself to be calm. "Congratulations, Anne." He couldn't quite bring himself to ask her how she felt about it. Memories of Ryan's conception and the fights they had had over their second child stood in the way of his being a totally nice guy. He wished he could have risen to the occasion, but he had long ago stopped trying to be perfect.

"I was thinking...I'm not quite sure how I'm going to tell Michael and Ryan."

He knew what was coming, and this time was having no part of it. But he stalled for time. "Anne, it's not as if you have to tell them tomorrow. You've still got some time to think about how you'll break it to them. They're good kids. They'll come around to accepting it. They'll just need some time."

He heard a soft sigh, then silence, and knew from long experience that she was gearing up to ask him. His instincts were correct.

"I thought you might want to tell them. I mean, you've been closer to them for all this time and it might hurt them less. I really don't want to hurt any of you anymore, Burt."

He had talked about Anne at length with Jerry. She was a passively aggressive woman, and his therapist friend had helped him see the predictable patterns in the way she had manipulated him. She had played the quintessential female to his all-protective male. Their "dances," as Jerry had referred to their self-destructive methods of behavior with each other, had meshed perfectly. Until all that perfection had blown up in their faces.

Now he was aware of it. He operated from a position of strength and knew how to deal with her.

"I really think you would hurt them more if you let them hear it through me. I think they're going to need you to reassure them that this baby doesn't mean you love them any less." He thought of the last time she had visited them, three months ago. Anne and her new husband lived in Newport Beach. It was a couple of hours away by car. Yet she claimed her schedule was so hectic...

As Sandy had gently lectured him when he had tried to get out of Wadsworth's training sessions, it was all a matter of setting priorities.

He might not be able to control how she hurt their children, but he didn't have to be a party to it.

"But I won't be able to make it up there for a while."

"You have plenty of time yet, Anne. You might just relax and get used to the idea yourself. Have you spoken to your mother lately?" He liked Anne's mother. Elizabeth Dearden—Betsy—had seen through her daughter's benign front, and had fought with her husband over the ways he had failed to discipline her. Betsy had been furious when faced with the fact that her only child was pregnant. But in time, after he and Anne married, Burt knew she had come to respect him. She had even taken his side in the divorce and had been one of the major reasons he had gained custody. Betsy phoned the boys weekly from her home in Connecticut, and had come to see them several times since the divorce.

"No, I . . . Well, it's no secret that she doesn't care for Carter. She was always so crazy about you."

Dangerous ground. Whenever Anne's life was shaky, she seemed to remember selectively, only the good times. The first few times he had believed her, let her tear up his guts with false hopes. Never again.

"Well, I'm crazy about her, so that makes us even."

He kept the conversation impersonal until Anne wound down, then after they hung up, he stared at the far wall of his bedroom. Betsy had commissioned a portrait of Anne and the boys for him as a Christmas present one year, and though he had disposed of many of the things he and Anne had collected together as a couple, he hadn't been able to part with the portrait. Partly because it was from Betsy, and partly because the artist had been talented. She had captured both boys' innocence, and even the sweetness in Anne that had attracted him to her in the first place.

He had wanted to protect her.

Now he stared at the picture, his entire body tense. Something was wrong. He had a feeling he had just seen the tip of the iceberg, but the rest was still hidden beneath very murky water.

"SO THE SWIMSUIT WORKED." Elaine was smugly triumphant.

"I was mad at you in the bathroom after I figured out you'd ditched the other swimsuit, but you were right." Sandy stretched in the lounge chair by the pool. She and Elaine were spending a lazy Sunday afternoon outside. She had worked with two dogs this morning, and was taking the rest of the day off.

It was a hot, clear summer day, and the profusion of brilliantly colored flowers Elaine had had planted around the house was so bright it almost hurt to look at them. Sandy kept her attention on the cool, blue surface of the pool. She smiled as Panda, her black mutt, trotted around the far side of the pool, her plumed tail waving.

"So, what are you going to do next?" Elaine asked, rolling over onto her stomach.

"I told him I'd call."

"Give him a few days."

"Why?"

"I saw this discussion on dating on *The Oprah Winfrey Show*. They say guys need time to fantasize about a woman. I'd give it a few days."

"I don't want to play any games with Burt, Elaine."

"Come on. There's no such thing as a male-female relationship without games. I've never heard of it."

"He's had too many games played on him already."

"Has he told you about his wife?"

"No. But just the fact that she gave Ryan such a huge dog. And Michael is so withdrawn. And Burt— Elaine, I can't put it all together so that it makes any sense, but I just feel he's really hurting."

"Yeah. What kind of woman gives up her kids, that's what I'd like to know."

"That's not fair. You don't know what kind of pressures she was under. It's that old walk-a-mile-in-her-moccasins thing—I don't want to pass any kind of judgment on her. I'm just picking up on what I see when I'm there. And it's not a good feeling."

"But his wife has nothing to do with you using your feminine wiles."

"The swimsuit was one thing, Elaine. I'm going to play it straight with him from now on. I'm sure that's what he needs."

"And what do you need?" Elaine eyed her shrewdly.

Sandy met her gaze with steady eyes. "I've never settled for anything less than one hundred percent from a man. I don't think Burt's going to disappoint me."

SHEBA WAS EVERYTHING *John had ever wanted in a woman. Sleek, calm, good in an emergency, she was next to him now, every muscle alert and tensed. Both watched the door, waiting for it to open. Knowing when it did, they wouldn't have much time.*

He could depend on Sheba. She would never betray him.

Burt grimaced as he stared at the screen.

Calm down. It's a rough draft. No one expects brilliant prose first time out. Keep going. It'll get better after a while.

He'd called Sandy this morning and asked for another session off. She'd agreed, understanding the pressure he was under. She was due to arrive within fifteen minutes, and he knew she would simply let herself into the kitchen and get Wadsworth's leash, then begin the training session.

She'd called him Sunday night. They'd talked on the phone for almost an hour, easy talk, touching base, teasing. He'd thought of asking her out to dinner, but something had stopped him. He liked the informal quality of their visits, and wanted to keep things as they were for just a little longer.

Michael had deserted today's lesson as well, pronouncing Wadsworth's training "stupid." Burt knew Sandy's presence around the house was bothering his older son. Michael was still waiting for his mother to come back.

He was hurting. Burt leaned back in his chair as he remembered the argument he had stopped this morning. Ryan had been crying, and he had caught a look of grim satisfaction on Michael's face as he had entered his older son's bedroom.

Michael had blurted out his side instantly.

"I *hate* it when he gets into my things, Dad! Tell him he can't go in my room!"

Ryan had been incoherent, and rushed toward his father, grabbing his legs.

He had separated them, confined both to their respective rooms, then slowly unraveled what had happened. Michael was picking on his younger brother once again. Ryan had only wanted one of his old toy trucks. Burt knew this streak of meanness was the only sense of power Michael had, but he didn't like the turn his older son's personality was taking. He was ugly around his brother when Burt wasn't there to supervise.

He sighed, saved his work, then turned off the computer. Once his mind was on his children and their problems, he found it impossible to write. Determined to discipline himself, he decided he would make himself a quick sandwich, then head back to his studio and work even if what he wrote would be good for nothing but the wastebasket.

He was getting out the mayonnaise when he heard Sandy's voice.

"Hi, Michael. Hi, Ryan."

"Hi, Sandy!" Ryan piped up. Michael didn't answer.

She was opening the gate to the backyard. The kitchen of the ranch-style house was along the driveway, and Burt managed a glimpse of strawberry-blond hair before he walked determinedly back to the refrigerator and pulled out Italian salami and provolone cheese.

"Hi, Burt." Sandy had walked into the kitchen through the back door. He turned, food in hand. She had Wadsworth's leash in her own. For a moment they simply stared, then Sandy smiled.

"Writing must build up an appetite."

"Yeah." Sometimes he was just befuddled by her. It was amazing how he could usually put a coherent thought on paper but couldn't come up with something clever to say.

"I hope the writing goes well today," she said softly, then turned to go.

"Sandy."

She stopped.

"Come by my office when you're done. Maybe we could make some lunch and talk."

"I'd like that." Then she was out the door, all long legs and gleaming, tousled hair.

He stared after her, remembering he'd decided to ask her how old she was. Maybe she just looked young. He had to try to understand the strange feelings of guilt he had when he thought of having any sort of serious relationship with her. After all, Anne had remarried. He certainly wasn't waiting around for her.

He walked slowly to the back door and watched as she took Wadsworth to the far end of the yard. The large sheepdog trotted obediently at her side. Burt knew they were working on "down" and "stay" today. He'd never been able to get the rambunctious dog to stay anywhere for longer than a second.

Burt watched Sandy for a moment longer, then returned to the counter. He reached into the cabinet for the bag of French rolls and was gently pulling one apart when he heard Michael's voice float up to the window from the driveway below.

"Nobody wants you to come along, that's why! You're just a baby!"

"No!" Ryan sounded desperate. "Daddy said I could go!"

"But I don't want to watch you, so you have to stay here."

Burt closed his eyes, set the roll down. He hated the tone in Michael's voice. He was going to have to call Jerry about this. Maybe he and Michael could go in for a few sessions together.

"You're too slow on your bike. Nobody wants to wait for you." Burt looked out the window over the sink in time to see Michael open the gate and wheel his bike outside. Ryan was standing still, watching his brother.

"Big baby. I knew you'd cry."

All thoughts of food forgotten, Burt headed toward the back door. He would comfort Ryan now and let Michael go on his bike hike. It might help him work off some of his anger. But he was going to have to talk to his older son tonight.

As he reached the back door, he heard a familiar voice and stopped.

"Ryan, I'm so glad you're here. It just so happens I need a helper. I didn't want to have to bother your dad, and Wadsworth's being a little difficult. Could you help me out?"

Bless you, Sandy. Burt started to smile.

"What do I do?" Ryan sounded unsure of himself, but intrigued.

"I'm trying to get him to stay. What I thought we could do is, I'll hold his collar and you run to the other end of the yard. I'll tell Wadsworth to stay, and when I give you a signal, call him to come. Okay?"

"Okay!"

And Burt knew all thoughts of the bike hike had flown out of his younger son's head.

He finished making his sandwich, then cleaned the kitchen and returned to his studio, determined to get

John Savage and Sheba out of their current predicament by the time Wadsworth's lesson was over.

HE WAS SAVING the last of the chapter when Ryan burst into his studio.

"Daddy, I made Wadsworth stay!" Ryan launched himself into his father's arms.

"I think that's great! After such hard work, you must be hungry."

"I am!"

Sandy was leaning in the doorway. He met her smile above his son's head. "I think we all worked pretty hard. How about McDonald's?"

"Chicken McNuggets!" Ryan yelled. "Can I bring some home for Wadsworth?"

"I think that might be arranged."

A half hour later he and Sandy were seated at an outdoor table, watching Ryan play in Ronald McDonald's park.

"Thanks for what you did with Ryan today."

"It was no problem. Wadsworth ran back toward the house and when I caught him I kind of overheard them. I felt sorry for Ryan. He was pretty upset."

Burt sighed, then helped himself to another of Sandy's French fries. He had already eaten all his own. "I'm going to have to talk to Michael."

"Do I make things worse?"

He admired the way she came straight to the point, no fooling around or dropping hints. "Michael resents any woman in the house who isn't his mother. You have nothing to do with it." His gaze followed Ryan's shout, and both he and Sandy watched as the little boy waved from the top of the giant hamburger.

"You have a lifelong friend in Ryan. I think he'd do anything for you."

"He's a great kid. So is Michael. You've done a good job with them, Burt."

He was comfortable with the compliment, knowing she wasn't trying to use it to gather information about his divorce. So many women he had dated had been surprised he had custody of his children. They had begun to ask questions instantly, wanting to know all the information. He liked the way Sandy seemed content to let things unfold at their own pace.

He remembered what he had wanted to ask her.

"How old are you, Sandy?"

She flashed him a mischievous grin. "Twenty-one."

He felt like a fool.

"I'm kidding. Twenty-six. I know I look young for my age. It's the freckles."

He swallowed, hard. He'd believed her. She wore little makeup, and her face had a freshness that was immensely appealing to him.

"How old are you?" she asked, reaching for another fry.

"Thirty-six."

"You were my age when Michael was born."

"Yeah." He felt infinitely old.

She seemed to sense his mood. He felt her loop her arm around his. "You don't kiss like an old man." Now she was teasing.

"Thirty-six isn't old," he informed her.

"You seem to think so."

He glanced over and caught sight of Ryan. "Does it bother you?"

"Nope. Should it?"

"I guess not." He glanced away as he asked the next question. "Are you going out with anyone right now?"

"You mean dating?"

"Yeah."

"No. Do you date?"

"I hate it."

"How come?"

"I don't know—it just makes me so uncomfortable. Maybe it's the women I've been seeing. I was with Anne for almost ten years. I guess I just got used to being a husband. The women I went out with—I couldn't stand it."

He caught a puzzled expression on her face, and instantly thought she must be wondering why he was telling her these things. Searching for the right words, he attempted to articulate his feelings.

"I want...I want to get to know you better, Sandy. I guess what I'm trying to say is that if I'm not any good at some of these dating things, I hope you'll take it in stride."

"You want to know a secret?"

"What?"

"I'm not very good at it either."

"You?" He was sure his incredulity showed on his face.

"Honest to God. I like to meet people, I like to go to parties and talk to a lot of people, but it seems like dating—I don't know. It's like you couldn't set up a more awkward situation for two people."

"My feelings exactly."

"Sometimes it's been hard for me because—I think guys have these expectations of me because of the way

I look. The tall blonde kind of thing, the California girl on the beach, the athletic type. A lot of the guys I went out with didn't give me credit for having anything upstairs.'' She took a deep breath. "I like talking with you, Burt. You treat me like I have a brain."

He slowly eased his arm away from her, reached out and encircled her shoulders, then squeezed. "I really like you, Sandy. But I'm still kind of scared. Can you understand that?"

"Perfectly."

"I don't want you to think I have no interest in you if I don't ask you out right away."

"I know."

"I must sound like a first-class fool."

"An honest one."

He caught the twinkle in her eye, threw back his head and laughed.

They were still laughing when Ryan rushed up to them, towing a clearly less-than-composed Cici. Ryan had been playing hard, and his hair stood out all over his head in sweaty spikes. His T-shirt was stained with ketchup and mustard, but his eyes were bright.

"Look, Daddy, it's Cici!"

"I was just walking home, Burt, and Ryan saw me."

"Cici, when can I come fill up the holes—"

"Ryan, Cici will let you know when you can come over. It's not polite to keep asking."

Ryan fell silent, then let go of Cici's hand, walked over and sat down next to his father.

Sandy seemed uneasy. "I'm going to get a sundae. Do you want one, Burt?"

"I do!" Ryan said. "With nuts."

"Burt, you know the ice cream here is made up of nothing but petroleum products." Cici turned her attention to Sandy. "How can you eat that?"

Burt saw the mischief in Sandy's eyes. "I can handle it, Cici. I'm a quart low, anyway."

"I'll have one too," Burt decided.

"And me!" Ryan said.

Sandy disappeared inside the restaurant, and Burt turned his attention back to his neighbor. "Has Wadsworth been giving you any trouble, Cici?"

"No. I have to admit, Cindy has been doing an excellent job."

"Sandy," Ryan said.

"Well, I've got a lot to do at home." Cici smiled. "It was nice to see you, Burt."

"You too, Cici."

When Sandy returned with three sundaes, Ryan announced, "I don't like Cici anymore."

"Ryan, I don't want you to say anything impolite to her."

"I don't like Cici. I like Sandy. Do you like Sandy, Daddy?"

He knew his smile was embarrassed as he glanced at her. He could feel the slightest warmth in his cheeks. But he met that steady gaze with his own.

"Yes, I do. A lot."

Chapter Five

"Thinking about the big B again?" Elaine teased.

Sandy jerked back to the present with a start. She and Elaine and Fred were enjoying a leisurely Sunday brunch out by the pool. It was a smoggy day, but this high up in the Hollywood Hills the air was clearer. The view of the city from Elaine's house was spectacular; you could see all the way from Hollywood to Century City, from the Capitol Record building to ABC's Entertainment Center. The Los Angeles skyline was marred only by a faint wash of brown pollution.

"I'm sorry." She reached for a chocolate croissant. "What were we talking about?"

"What else?" Fred settled back in his chair, balancing a cup of coffee in his long-fingered hands. "The Big L."

"Love. Hmm." She bit into the croissant.

"You're certainly in a good mood," Elaine observed.

Sandy nodded her head.

"Has Burt asked you out yet?"

She shook her head and swallowed.

"Aren't you worried?"

"No. Burt and I understand each other."

"Isn't that pretty boring?" asked Fred. He was constantly in the clutches of one little girl groupie after another, though Sandy privately thought that the woman who could handle Fred just hadn't come along yet. She was looking forward to the day.

"No. I really like what we have."

"And what is that?" Elaine asked.

"An . . . understanding."

Fred rolled his eyes. "Well, if you're so content, then help Ellie and me. We were just trying to figure out when you know it's really the big one. I know when it's *not* love."

"And when's that?" Sandy asked.

"When," Fred said mournfully, "she fixes you instant coffee instead of regular. Then it's all over."

"Oh, please," Elaine shot back. "The pubescent types that send your hormones raging don't even know how to cook. They've barely packed away their dolls."

"Ellie, Ellie," Fred said soothingly, "they're all legal age. They have to be to get into the clubs."

Sandy reached for another croissant and watched her roommates snap verbal zingers back and forth across the glass-topped table. Her mind wandered, and suddenly she wondered if Elaine and Fred would ever admit to having feelings for each other besides friendship.

The thought was so outrageous she broke into a grin.

"What's so funny?" Elaine asked as she poured herself her fifth cup of coffee. Her friend lived a frenetic, fast-paced existence and consumed enormous quantities of caffeine to keep herself going.

"I was thinking about Cici," Sandy lied, not wanting either Elaine or Fred to be aware of the workings of her mind.

"The Stepford Cici?" Fred quipped. "I'd like to meet this woman. Perhaps she's the one—"

"I don't think so." Now Sandy was really grinning. She could just picture Cici's expression if she answered the door and found Fred, with his longish hair and boyish charm, on her doorstep. No, there was only one man in the greater Los Angeles area that Cici wanted to get her hands on.

"Well," Elaine said, cutting an almond croissant in half with her knife, "what do you have planned for the big B? Even if the two of you've reached an understanding and he hasn't asked you out, that doesn't mean you can't do anything to change the situation." She picked up half the croissant and bit into it.

Sandy had some plans, but she didn't want to share them with her friends just yet. She decided to change the subject.

"How do you define love, Elaine?"

"I'm in love when . . ." Elaine pretended to be deep in thought, and Sandy knew she was going to make a joke to cover up her true feelings on the subject. "When I shave my legs twice a day."

Sandy laughed, then reached for the coffeepot.

"I have one last question," Fred said.

"What?" Elaine replied.

"Why do women always cut croissants in half and eat little bites when they know they're going to eat the other half anyway?"

"Fred," Elaine said with mock disdain, "a gentleman would never bring up such a subject."

BURT HAD HIS TALK with Michael Sunday morning. His son had come in looking so tired from his biking that he hadn't the heart to hit him with some serious discipline. So Burt waited. After breakfast, he and Ryan drove down to the corner 7-Eleven and bought a Sunday paper and some comic books. Then Burt waited until Ryan fell asleep, and carried his younger son into his bedroom and tucked him in.

When he came back into the den, Michael was lying on his stomach reading the comics.

"Michael?"

His son looked up, and Burt felt the same little pang he always experienced when he studied his older son's face. He looked so much like Anne. The same sweetness was there, the same perfect balance of features. The light brown, straight hair that the sun shot with gold. The light blue, intelligent eyes surrounded by darker lashes. The same straight nose, classic chin and good cheekbones.

"Yeah?"

"I'd like us to talk, okay?"

"Okay." He was already wary.

"Are you feeling all right these days?"

He could see his son shutting down, right before his eyes. Whatever Michael was feeling, he didn't want the world to know.

"Yeah, I'm fine."

"The other day, about Ryan and the bike ride—"

"Dad, he's just too little! I *hate* it when he tags along! None of the other guys have little brothers they have to drag along with them everywhere they go!"

"Do I really ask you to take Ryan with you all the time?" The question was voiced in a soft tone. Remembering his own father, Burt tried to steer the conversation toward a practical solution.

Michael hesitated for a moment, then said, "Not all the time, I guess."

"Would it have killed you to have let Ryan go along yesterday?"

Now Michael was looking at the floor, and as much as Burt wanted to see the expression in his son's eyes, he wouldn't command him to look up at him.

"Not really, I guess."

"Do the other guys tease you about having to take Ryan along?"

"Sometimes, but I don't mind that much. It isn't really Ryan that much, Dad, it's—" He stopped.

It's Sandy. It's Anne. It's everything that's happened to him that never should have happened.

"It's . . ." he prompted gently.

"It's nothing, Dad. I'll try to be better with Ryan."

"Okay. And Michael?"

"Yeah?"

"Will you talk to me if anything else is bugging you?"

"Yeah, I will, Dad. Can I go back to reading the comics now?"

He smiled. "Okay."

Burt lay down on the leather couch and closed his eyes. It was pleasant, lying quietly and listening to the soft rustle of newspaper as Michael quickly turned the comic pages. Both his children liked to read. He was thankful for that.

He could hear Wadsworth barking faintly outside in the yard. With Ryan asleep and Michael next to him stretched out on the floor, Burt allowed himself to revel in the peace and security. That was one thing positive the divorce had done for him—he never took these moments for granted.

The phone call from Anne hovered at the edge of his thoughts. He was still bothered by it, but he didn't know why. He wondered if Carter would have as much trouble convincing Anne to continue her pregnancy as he had when she had been pregnant with Ryan—if Carter would even care the way he had.

He was almost asleep when the phone rang.

"Do you want me to get it, Dad?"

"Thanks, Michael. Could you take a message?"

But his son was back within the minute. "It's Nana. She wants to talk to you."

Betsy. Anne's mother. And when Betsy summoned you to the phone, you answered that summons.

Burt walked into the kitchen, then picked up the phone and sat down at the oak table.

"Hello, Betsy. How are you?" He could picture Anne's mother. Betsy should have run the corporation, not her husband, Kent. She was the tougher of the two. Anne had never been able to manipulate her mother the way she had her father. Betsy's sharp blue eyes took in everything. She would be sitting by the phone now dressed impeccably, hair done, her cigarettes close at hand.

"Burt. How are you and the boys?"

"Fine."

"Good. Did my daughter tell you she was pregnant?"

How like Betsy, to get straight to the point. He had never wasted a second with his mother-in-law on the phone. "Yes. She called me."

"I hope you understand what this means."

His grip on the phone tightened. Sudden instinct told him he was about to come face-to-face with the dark underside of that iceberg.

"She's going to demand custody of the children."

Everything within him went perfectly still. There was a bee buzzing in the sweet peas outside the large kitchen window, and the noise sounded loud inside the kitchen. That and the ticking of the clock above the stove.

He forced himself to stay calm, forced the words out of his throat. "I can't believe Anne would do that. Not after all Michael and Ryan have been through." He spoke quietly, not wanting his older son to overhear.

"Burt, you have consistently underestimated my daughter. Don't make the same mistake again."

He took a deep breath. "What do you think I should do?"

She didn't hesitate. "I've talked to Jim Fenhagen. California custody laws are some of the toughest in the country. You'll have to fight harder this time, Burt, and fight dirty. I'm just calling to prepare you, and to tell you I'll support you every step of the way."

He was silent, taking this all in. One phone conversation had destroyed all the peace and security he had worked so desperately to achieve.

"I know my daughter better than anyone else," Betsy said with quiet conviction. "And I know what she's capable of." He heard her take a deep drag of her cigarette. She exhaled, then continued. "You know I didn't like you in the beginning, Burt. I thought you were...irresponsible. But when I visited you last Easter, I saw my grandsons happy, and that's all that matters to me anymore. Anne can make what she wants of her life, but I will not have those children destroyed. They've been hurt enough.''

His eyes stung, his throat closed. It was beginning to sink in, and he knew Betsy was telling him the truth. It was only a matter of time before Anne called.

''She's crazy enough when she isn't pregnant. Now that she's going to have this Carter's child, she'll want to reunite the whole family. Get a pencil, Burt. I want you to take down Jim's number. Call him. He'll find you the best lawyer in Southern California. You'll need someone excellent. The natural mother has every advantage.''

Fingers numb, he reached for a pencil.

SANDY LAY BACK in the bathtub and luxuriated in the silky bubbles. Elaine had gone out with Fred to The Improv, one of Los Angeles's hottest comedy clubs. She had the house to herself, and it suited her mood. She needed time to think.

Her mind drifted as she soaked in the tub. The bathroom was dark except for the light of three squat white candles in Indian brass candleholders. She had perched one on a chair by the bathtub, one up by the sink and one on the toilet tank. The softly gleaming brass candleholders had designs cut in their sides, in diamond and heart shapes, so patterns of light danced across the smooth white stucco walls.

She turned her head at the slight sound at the door. ''Come on in, Panda.''

Her dog, feathery tail wagging and crazy airplane ears cocked up, pushed the door open a little more and slipped inside. She trotted to the edge of the tub and swiped at Sandy's face with her tongue.

"That's a good girl, Panda," she crooned. "Now, down. Good girl."

Panda lay on her side, sighed, then closed her eyes.

Sandy sank down into the warm tub and stared at the ceiling.

She loved the feeling of being surrounded by water, did some of her best thinking in the tub. Now she relaxed, closing her eyes but not at all sleepy. She felt as if her awareness were heightened.

The past few weeks, since meeting Burt, had been hectic. Her feelings had raced along, she had thought about him so much. Now it was time to slow down and look deep within.

Whenever she wanted to put her feelings in perspective, she thought of her brother. Elaine knew her twin had died four years ago. Sandy didn't know whether she had told Fred. She herself rarely told anyone. Jimmy's death had been a turning point in her life. She still talked to him, when she could find a quiet moment. Just before she went to bed. Early in the morning when the sun was rising. Sometimes she talked out loud while she drove, but mostly it was a dialogue she carried on within her head.

She never spoke to anyone about it because she was afraid they would think she was crazy. Yet she sometimes had very strong feelings and knew Jimmy was close. And she trusted those instincts.

She kept her brother's picture by her bed, but even without the visual reminder she could never forget her twin's face. He hadn't looked like her. They had both been tall, but Jimmy had had dark hair and blue eyes like their father. Sandy took after their mother.

Now as she soaked in the warm, fragrant water, she thought of his face, especially his smile. The first thought slipped easily into her consciousness.

You'd like him, Jimmy. A lot. He has the same . . . sense of caring. Sometimes when he smiles, he reminds me of you, the way his eyes stay serious. It takes a little to get him to laugh, but when he does, it makes me feel so good.

He's a good dad. His kids are terrific. Michael is ten, Ryan's five. And the dog—Wadsworth—is a real character. Remember Mrs. Malone's dog, Catcher? Wadsworth looks like him.

She felt totally at peace, soaking in the tub, the candlelight flickering over the walls, the bath foam and melting candle wax scenting the air.

Sometimes he seems so sad. I don't think I came into his life at a good time, Jimmy. If I could wish for perfect conditions—If I could, you'd still be here with me, wouldn't you? But with Burt—I wish sometimes so badly that I could have met him at a different time. I don't mean when he was younger. I just mean when he didn't have so much on his mind.

She let her mind wander, knowing the right thought would come effortlessly.

I know about love. I know I love you, and Mom and Dad and Bo. What I feel for Burt, it's developing into the same type of love, but different. Sometimes I think, if I were really strong, I could give up ever having a chance to love Burt if all the pain would just leave him. It's not that he's frightened. It's just that— you know how you once said there were times you had been through so much you just couldn't feel any-more? That's what I get from him. He jokes around with me, but he's just kind of burned out. He gives to everyone else, but no one gives to him. His children love him, but I mean giving in an adult way.

She could feel the tears pricking beneath her eye-lids.

Jimmy, I want to give to him, but sometimes I wonder if it's just for selfish reasons, like for my own benefit. I love being with him. I never thought about his being ten years older until he brought it up. It never bothered me. I was aware of him from the first mo-ment I saw him. I can't explain it any better than that.

And Michael. The ten-year-old. I don't want to hurt him. So life's kind of a mess right now, and I keep thinking about how you always used to tell me to trust my feelings about things. And to dare.

I'm scared. Not that he doesn't feel the same way, but that so many things are going on that could come between these feelings. I don't even know what these things are, it's just a feeling I have. I know we just can't stand still, that I have to take a chance. I just have this feeling it has to come from me, and I don't want to make a mistake.

She could see her twin smiling in her mind's eye, the brilliant blue eyes dazzling. No one had eyes that saw more than Jimmy's. In the end, after his death, she'd realized her twin had always seen more of the world's possibilities than anyone else.

I know—nothing ventured, nothing gained. And there is only this moment. And life is never perfect. I guess I always knew it all along, but it's just good to talk to you.

I'm going to go now. I'll talk to you soon. Take care of yourself.

Her eyes stung.

I miss you. And I love you.

Sandy opened her eyes, and the bathroom looked sharper, clearer. Her mind felt rested, her body relaxed. Panda was sleeping, breathing softly.

"Are you happy, Jimmy?" she whispered softly.

The candlelight flickered, and she smiled.

"GOOD NIGHT, DAD." Michael looked so small in his bed as Burt leaned over and kissed him good-night. Then he straightened slowly and walked out of the bedroom.

He'd already tucked Ryan in. They were so different, his sons. Ryan still had his Winnie-the-Pooh curtains and bedspread. He had picked them out himself, on a shopping expedition at Sears. Stuffed animals crammed every shelf and were piled on his bed. Ryan was a real animal lover. He spent more time outside with Wadsworth now that the animal was somewhat trained, and talked constantly about Butch, the hamster at his playschool.

There was a Garfield poster taped to his closet door, and another of a koala bear by his bed. Ryan loved koala bears. Burt had given up trying to keep his room perfectly clean, and usually some toys and clothes littered the floor. He had a whole shelf of toy trucks, another of his passions.

Michael's room was completely different. He had his trophy shelf, and there were several trophies lined up already, from the various swim meets he had competed in. Michael drove himself, and Burt worried deeply about his older son's insistence on perfection. He saw the childlike fingernails bitten to the quick, the guarded look in his eyes.

A stuffed Garfield still graced one of the other shelves, but now most toys had been replaced by models, games and books. Michael loved planes, and a huge model plane hung from his ceiling. Burt could still remember the day he had put the hook in the ceiling. There was a small table in the corner, with a diorama for school on top for it, along with the microscope Burt had given him for Christmas last year. The usual assortment of footballs and basketballs littered the floor by his closet, along with wadded-up jeans and T-shirts. Lately Michael's room was so messy you could barely open the door.

On the table by Michael's bed was a framed photo he had chosen from the collection in the den. It had been taken on his seventh birthday. He and Anne had treated Michael to Disneyland for the day. Betsy had stayed home with Ryan. He and Anne actually looked happy. Michael, in Mickey Mouse ears, stood between them, a huge grin on his face and a stuffed Dumbo in his arms.

Burt had taken every framed photo out of his bedroom and put them on the shelves in the den. He rarely glanced at the pictures, didn't like to remember the way Anne looked. But he couldn't erase her presence. It wouldn't have been fair to his children. Still, he thought it was telling that Michael had chosen that particular picture.

Maybe we should go to Disneyland again. But the minute he thought of the idea, he dismissed it. Michael wouldn't want to have Ryan tagging after him.

Burt considered taking Michael and a few of his friends, but his elder son didn't seem to want to have too much to do with him, either.

One of the saddest things he had learned was that he could not recapture moments. That day at Disneyland was one of the happiest they had spent as a family. It was no mistake Michael had that photo by his bed.

Burt thought of going into his studio and trying to make sense of the book he had partially on disc, then decided against it. He'd start again in the morning. He thought of a solitary cup of coffee and watching the news later on, but found he was exhausted. Slowly, he made his nightly round of the house, making sure Wadsworth was inside and all the doors were locked. Then he left the night-light burning in the hall bathroom and retired to his bedroom.

He took a long, hot shower, but it failed to relieve the tension in his muscles. He hadn't been fully relaxed since Betsy's warning. Burt knew his mother-in-law was right: it was only a matter of time before Anne called. He felt he and the boys were suspended in time, inside this peaceful house, but it was only a matter of weeks before their world was ripped inside out. Perhaps even days.

The summer evening was warm, but not hot enough to warrant turning on the air conditioner. Dressed only in his pajama bottoms, he lay in bed on top of the covers and stretched, trying to find a comfortable position and perhaps sleep.

The third time he glanced at the clock, almost an hour had passed.

At two-thirty in the morning the phone rang. He picked up the receiver swiftly, his stomach tensed. There was only one person who called this late at night.

"Burt? Is that you?" It was Anne, her soft voice slightly slurred.

"Annie? Are you all right?" She drank when she was unhappy, so he knew this pregnancy wasn't a happy one, either.

"I'm fine. Burt, I'm so tired. I couldn't sleep, so I decided to call you. Maybe you couldn't sleep, either. Do you remember?" Her voice was sleepy, but still playful.

He stared at the ceiling, tension knotting his neck and shoulders. At twenty-six, they had both been ignorant enough to confuse intense sexual chemistry with lasting love. Yet he had felt so strongly about Anne, truly loved her in the early years.

He and Anne had shared a tendency to insomnia, and had both laughed at their inability to sleep. They had spent many nights together, awake, in bed. Before the last two years of their marriage, when they still made love regularly, those long nights had not been wasted. Neither of them had come to the marriage a virgin, and the chemistry between them, coupled with knowledge, had created countless erotic encounters.

"Do you?" she asked sleepily.

"Does Carter know you're drinking?" he asked. Burt had never met the man, and now felt sorry for him. He wondered if Carter had known what he was getting involved with.

"He's in bed," Anne whispered. "I missed you so I wanted to call."

I missed. I wanted. Some things never changed.

"Do you miss me?" she said, then laughed softly.

He swallowed, hard. "Anne, don't drink while you're pregnant."

"Carter's not a strong man," she replied, as if she hadn't heard what he'd said. "Not like you. Burt, do you remember that night we had the fight over at my mother's house? You remember, the summer Michael was three. You were so mad, I made you so mad—"

"Anne, stop it—"

"And you picked me up over your shoulders and carried me back to our room and then—" She stopped suddenly, and he heard her sigh. "I miss that, Burt. You were a son of a bitch in some ways, but there was never a man who could get me as crazy as you could."

He couldn't answer her. Anne would throw back her head and laugh if she knew he hadn't been with a woman since the divorce. The first year, emotionally numb, he had hardly thought about sex at all. During the past six months he'd dated, but besides being discreet for the boys' sake, he hadn't met a woman who had meant that much to him.

Until Sandy.

He had to change the subject. Anne was driving him crazy. As bad as they had been for each other in the end, she knew him as no other woman did. She had been an adventurous sexual partner, had pushed him to his limits. As bitter as their divorce had been, he'd been shocked to find he still sometimes dreamed about her. There was nothing as safe as the familiar.

"What did you have to drink?" he asked. He wasn't jealous that his ex-wife was carrying another man's child, but he thought of that child now, and of the disadvantage Anne was saddling it with.

"Scotch. A little. Carter will never know. He doesn't know me like you do, Burt."

He could hear the smile in her voice. Burt glanced at the clock. He'd been talking to her for less than five minutes, and she had ripped into him again, making him a little bit crazy, making him think of all they had shared. He knew Anne's mind. She didn't want to be married to him, but she didn't want him to have a life away from her.

He thought of sinking to her level, of hurting her and telling her he had met a woman he thought he might be able to care for far more than he had ever cared for her. But he remembered what Betsy had said, and knew he had to proceed with caution. He didn't want Anne to become any more depressed than she already was.

This new marriage was certainly a mistake, as was the pregnancy. The last thing he wanted to do was help her along in her misery. Then she would turn on her two children as a means of relieving her suffering, convincing herself if she had them back all would be well.

He hadn't lived with her for almost ten years and not figured out how her mind worked. But not as well as her mother had, or he would have seen trouble coming a long time ago.

Now he relied on the tried and true. How well he knew the dance.

"It hurts me to hear you like this, Anne. Why don't you go on back to Carter and try to lie down?" His voice was soft and soothing.

"I don't sleep in Carter's room anymore," she said, her voice fading in and out.

"Where are you now?" he asked.

"Lying on the sofa."

If she fell asleep, at least she wouldn't hurt herself. "Annie, hang up the phone and stay there on the couch. You have to rest. You have to take care of the baby."

"That's all you ever cared about, the damned babies." Her voice was fainter now, and he knew the conversation was nearing its end.

"That's not true. I loved you." Burt had no trouble with telling her the truth. He had told her he loved her often enough when they had been married.

"I made a mistake, Burt, leaving you." She was winding down, the words following their familiar pattern. It wouldn't be long now.

"Put the phone down, Anne. Hang it up and go to sleep." His voice was low and soothing.

"Will you do one more thing for me?" It was barely a whisper.

He knew what it was. "Sure."

"Call me baby. The way you used to after we..." Her voice drifted off.

"Go to sleep, baby. Go to sleep."

"I did love you, Burt. I loved you but I messed it all up. I'm sorry."

"Go to sleep, Annie."

She hung up the phone and he listened to the dial tone for a few seconds before he replaced the receiver in its cradle. Burt lay in the darkened bedroom, his arm over his eyes. His stomach hurt, his chest felt tight. He felt totally drained. And totally depressed.

Then he got up quietly and walked toward the bathroom, knowing he was going to be sick.

Chapter Six

Sandy was in the midst of teaching Wadsworth "go to
your place," when she heard the gate slam, then fran-
tic footsteps by the side of the house. As the place Burt
had decided upon for Wadsworth was by the back
steps, when Ryan came tearing around the corner he
ran right into her.

"Whoa, what happened, Ryan?"

His jeans and Get-Along Gang T-shirt were
drenched with water and his wet hair stood up in
spikes all over his head. There were angry tears standing out in his eyes as he looked at her. Sandy had been
kneeling beside Wadsworth, so they were on eye level.

"I'm dead! They killed me!"

"Who killed you?"

"Michael. He didn't want me in the game, so he
killed me."

"What game?"

"Killer."

"How did they kill you?"

"With a water balloon. Now I'm dead, and I can't
play for the rest of the game."

"That's a problem." Sandy released Wadsworth's collar and gave him a playful pat on the rump. The sheepdog trotted to the far end of the yard and began to roll in the grass, scratching his shaggy back.

"What can we do that'll make things better?" Sandy asked. "I was just about finished with Wadsworth anyway, so now we can do something." She knew Burt was working furiously, and she didn't want to have to disturb him. There was something bothering him. He'd told her he was determined to get this book finished ahead of schedule. It was almost as if he wanted to put it behind him and be ready for other things.

"We could go inside and watch *Star Wars*," Ryan said hopefully.

"I think I can figure out your VCR."

"And we could have ice cream."

She stared down at him and Ryan started to laugh. She was well aware of his manipulations, and wasn't about to fall for this latest ploy.

"Have you even had lunch?"

"No."

"Don't you think we should save the ice cream for after lunch?"

"I guess so."

It was hot outside, and she welcomed the air-conditioned interior of the sprawling, ranch-style house. Sandy poured both herself and Ryan glasses of fruit punch. The temperature was up in the nineties today, so she'd been careful not to overexert Wadsworth. She peeked out the back window and saw the sheepdog lying in the enormous hole he had dug in the shade of the grapefruit tree. She had cautioned Burt not to punish the dog for holes like these—Wadsworth was just trying to beat the intense heat, and the freshly dug earth would provide him with a cool place to lie down.

"Can we have sandwiches and Cheetos?" Ryan asked, fruit punch staining his mouth.

"Sure. C'mere." She handed him a dish towel, the corner dampened. "Wipe your mouth, okay?"

He did as she asked, then scooted up on a kitchen chair and watched as she took bread and lunch meat out and placed them on the counter. Burt had made it quite clear that she was to have free access to the refrigerator, and this wasn't the first time she had made Ryan lunch. Now, Sandy sensed a quiet desperation to Burt, and she wanted to assist in any small way she could. Keeping Ryan fed and entertained would help.

"Why don't you change into dry clothes while I finish making lunch?" she suggested.

Ryan was off his chair immediately, and she could hear him thundering down the hall toward his room.

When he came back a short time later, in red shorts and a navy blue tank top, Sandy had placed their lunch on a tray in the den and was studying the VCR, the *Star Wars* tape in hand. The film ran around two hours, and Burt would be finished working by then. Michael was out of the house, as usual, so with luck Burt wouldn't be disturbed.

Ryan bounded onto the couch and reached for one of the sandwiches.

Convinced she knew what she was doing, Sandy inserted the tape and turned on both the VCR and the television. Then she walked back toward the couch and sat down next to Ryan. As the credits rolled and

Ryan ate, she sipped at her fruit punch. It had been so hot outside. She wasn't even really hungry. Setting her glass down, Sandy tipped her head back and closed her eyes.

She'd seen Burt briefly this morning. He'd been glad to see her, but she had sensed he was on edge. He'd begged off the session, and she had been quick to reassure him that she knew he'd been working hard with Wadsworth, so she could simply inform him of any new behavior she taught the sheepdog today. Wadsworth was much improved six weeks into his training.

She and Burt talked on the phone at least three times a week. Their conversations were still light, though a few times he had told her of his confusion in dealing with Michael. They had discussed Wadsworth—the first few times Burt had called, it had been on the pretense of asking her a question concerning dog training. From that point, they had talked of everything and anything.

Sandy was sure he cared about her. And she sensed he needed to take things slowly. There were times she wished they could go out together, but if Burt had his reasons for wanting to proceed with caution, she wasn't going to push him.

"Can I take the Cheetos by the TV?" Ryan asked, and Sandy opened her eyes and glanced down at the little boy. His hair was drying, and he had eaten a sandwich and drunk all his punch. He had the bowl of Cheetos in his lap.

"Sure. Ryan, I'm going to lie down for a little bit. If you need anything, wake me up. Don't disturb your dad, all right?"

"Okay."

She knew the odds were he wouldn't. Ryan watched *Star Wars* over and over; it was his favorite movie. He would be glued to the set for the next few hours. And since she only meant to snooze for about twenty minutes...

Her eyes drifted shut again, and she heard the sound of the dog door banging and Wadsworth's toenails clicking against the kitchen floor. Sandy slid down on the couch and kicked off her sneakers. She pillowed her cheek against the soft leather and gave herself up to sleep.

SANDY WOKE SLOWLY, slightly disoriented. The den was dark, the television set turned off. Ryan was nowhere to be seen.

She was about to sit up on the couch when she heard Michael's voice coming from the kitchen.

"Dad, why is she always here?" He sounded angry.

She froze, painfully aware she was eavesdropping. But if she made them both aware she was awake, it would only be worse.

"That's not fair, Michael. Sandy comes here on Saturdays to train Wadsworth. You know that."

"Yeah, she really looks like she's training Wadsworth now."

"Michael, Sandy is a friend of mine. You don't have to like her, but I expect you to respect her and make her feel she's welcome here."

"She's sleeping on the couch, Dad!"

"She was watching Ryan for me. She doesn't have to do that, Michael! That's not the reason she's here. But she's a good friend, so she's helping me."

There was a short silence. Sandy could feel a muscle in her leg cramping, and she bit her lip against the spasm, then stretched her leg out as silently as she could.

Michael's next question was asked in a tight, flat voice. "She's going to take Mom's place, isn't she?"

"No one will ever take over your mother's place, Michael. But you have to understand she isn't coming back here to live with us."

"Are you going to marry Sandy? Will she come here and live with us?"

She could hear Burt's sigh. "Michael."

She thought about how hard this question was going to be to answer, and wished with all her heart she was anywhere but where she was.

"I'm not going to lie to you, Michael. I don't want to confuse you. If you've been feeling that Sandy is special to me, you're right. But no one will ever take over your mother's place, or become your mom if you don't want it to happen. It doesn't work like that."

"But if you marry Sandy, maybe she wouldn't want Mom to come over."

"I don't think Sandy's like that."

There was a short silence.

"You liked her in the beginning," Burt said softly. "I remember you liked her motorcycle."

"It's dumb," Michael replied. "None of the other moms rides a cycle."

"When she first started training Wadsworth, you thought the lessons were pretty interesting."

"He's Ryan's dumb dog. I don't care anymore."

"Do you miss your mother?"

How like Burt, Sandy thought, *to go straight to the heart of the problem. It really does have nothing to do with anything but the fact that he misses his mother.* She had wondered why Burt's ex had never shown up on any of the Saturdays she had been at the house. Then she had decided that perhaps she came over on Sundays. But from the sound of this conversation, she decided it had been quite a while since Michael had seen his mother.

"I talked with her this afternoon," Burt said. "I meant to tell you as soon as you came home. She wants to come by and take you out to dinner, just the two of you."

"You mean not even Ryan?" Now Michael sounded happy.

"Nope. Just you."

"Wow, Dad, that's great! When?"

"Next Saturday. So you see, no one's taking your mother's place. Now, can you find it inside yourself to be nicer to Sandy?"

There was a short pause. "I guess so."

"Just don't be rude to her, okay?"

"Okay."

Sandy heard Michael's light footsteps as he left the kitchen, and she closed her eyes and feigned sleep as Burt entered the den.

She felt his finger lightly touch her cheek and she wrinkled her nose, then slowly woke, hoping he would be taken in by her performance.

But he must have seen something in her eyes.

"I'm sorry you had to hear that," Burt said softly.

"It's the truth."

"It's the truth for Michael. It's hard for him to understand."

"Maybe I shouldn't be around here all the time."

"All the time? I feel like I hardly see you. You're not with me, Sandy. You're out working with Wadsworth or taking care of Ryan, and speaking of which I'm going to figure that into your fee."

"No." She sat up on the couch, pushing her hair out of her eyes. "I take care of Ryan because I want to. I don't want to be paid for it."

"If you feel that strongly about it—"

"I do. It's not work. I like him, Burt." She put her hand on his arm. "I guess I'm just . . . scared. I don't know, Burt. Sometimes I feel selfish because I want time with you alone, but I know you have a book to finish and Michael and Ryan to consider. And I know there are other things on your mind."

It was there again, in his eyes. That clouded, faraway look. Just enough to let her know she had hit the truth.

He had been kneeling on the floor, and now he got up and sat down next to her. "I think you're right. We do need some time together."

"I don't want Michael to think I'm taking you away from him, Burt. I do understand, more than you think I do."

"I know. There's nothing that says we can't spend some time together here. I'll make the boys some supper, then once they're in bed, if you can stay with them for twenty minutes, I'll run down and rent a couple of videos and we can order a pizza." He hesitated. "It's a pretty shabby first date, but at least we'd be spending time together."

"It doesn't sound shabby at all. I'd love it. Just you and me and a couple of movies. It'll be like high school."

"If I can remember back that far." He tugged a lock of her hair gently, then smiled. "You're sure."

"It sounds fine."

Later, once the boys were both in bed and their food order had been phoned in, Burt left to pick up both the videos and the pizza. Sandy wandered back into the den. A single lamp cast a soft glow over the room. It was a masculine room, with the black leather couches and heavy glass coffee table. But the furniture wasn't what drew her attention. That was caught and held by the grouping of framed photos on the far bookshelf. Sandy found herself slowly walking over toward them.

She wanted to see what Burt's ex-wife looked like.

The photos had been carefully selected and framed. A wedding portrait: a much younger Burt, his hair a little longer, in a morning suit, his bride on his arm. Sandy didn't know what his wife's name was, but now she knew she was beautiful. Stunningly beautiful. This was the girl that graced Estee Lauder ads, the patrician nose and cheekbones, large expressive blue eyes, dark blond hair cut chin-length—a style only a beautiful woman could wear. She was a fairy-tale creature, in a gossamer web of silk and lace with a bouquet of orchids. And she was smiling directly at the photographer.

They were so beautiful together, it hurt to look at them. She recognized pride and love in Burt's eyes.

There was a sense of happiness to the photo, and as she looked at it she wondered what had gone wrong.

Her glance strayed to other pictures. Burt holding a tiny baby. It had to be Michael—Burt still looked so young. His wife sitting on the front steps of this house, Michael standing close to her. Burt sat next to them, Ryan held in his arms. He couldn't have been over a year old. Sandy studied Michael's face intently. He resembled his mother. And there were already signs of strain in the young boy's face. His eyes looked startled, even when he was smiling. Was the marriage already coming apart?

She felt she was eavesdropping again, only this time deliberately and in a much more personal way. There were a lot of pictures of Michael and Ryan, but the one that finally caught and held her attention was a single shot of Burt's wife. She was walking along the beach in a white sundress, sandals caught in her hand. It could have been a page out of a fashion magazine, and Sandy knew how hard photographers worked to achieve just the proper effect. This looked as if it had simply been snapped on the spur of the moment.

But it was the expression on the woman's face that arrested her. In Sandy's active imagination, this woman had everything. Looks, grace, elegance. A handsome husband, two beautiful boys. Yet there was something so sad, almost a haunted look in her eyes as she stared out at the waves. There was an air of sadness to the picture, but she couldn't quite define it.

The house was very still, so she heard Burt's car come gliding up the driveway. Not wanting to be caught snooping, Sandy moved away from the pictures and sat back down on the couch.

He walked into the den within minutes.

"I hope you like Woody Allen," he said as he laid the plastic bag containing the videos on the coffee table. He held the cardboard pizza box in his other hand, and the smell of pepperoni, fresh-baked pizza dough and Italian spices permeated the air.

"I love him. Which ones did you get?"

"*Annie Hall* and *Manhattan*." He set the box down on the coffee table. "Hang on, I'll get us some paper plates and napkins. Do you want wine or beer?"

"Wine's fine."

Soon they were sitting on the couch, the only light in the den from the large television screen.

Sandy found that the wine helped relax her. She finished three pieces of pizza, and as Burt opened the carton to get her a fourth, she shook her head.

"No more for me."

"I think I'm stuffed, too. Let's get comfortable."

The couch was large, with several squooshy leather pillows. As Burt lay down, he took Sandy's hand and gently pulled her down beside him so her back was to his chest and she could still see the television screen. His arm came around her waist, and he held her tightly against him.

She closed her eyes, infinitely content to be lying close to him. She could feel the warmth of his chest through his cotton shirt and her thin T-shirt. His arm felt hard and muscled against her stomach. Resting her head on one of the pillows, she listened to the dialogue without opening her eyes. She had seen *Annie Hall* so many times she could visualize what part of the movie was on the screen.

Toward the end, when Alvy and Annie were in the process of breaking up, she took Burt's hand in hers and pressed it against her stomach. Sometimes, when she rented the film, she only played it up to the part where they were still together, then rewound it.

But the film continued, and in the end, as always, she had tears in her eyes when the scenes of that very special courtship were played across the screen.

Burt reached for the remote control, shut off the tape, then started to rewind it. He lowered the volume on the television, then set the remote control down beside the half-empty bottle of wine.

"Are you up for another movie?"

She was feeling so warm and alive, so relaxed from the wine. Sandy slowly rolled over on the couch until she was facing him, her cheek pillowed on his arm.

"Maybe we could have a little intermission," she said softly.

"I like the way your mind works."

"It must be a conditioned reflex. You know, all those dates at the theater during high school. What else do you do at the movies?"

"Uh-huh." His face was very close to hers.

She wrinkled her brow in pretended concentration. "That is, if they had movies back when you were in high school...." She let her voice trail off, then smiled up at him.

"I'll have to get you for that." He leaned over her and kissed the side of her neck.

She caught her breath sharply, then reached up and gently ran her fingers through his hair. "Wasn't it silent pictures? Or maybe the talkies—"

He captured her mouth in a kiss so slow and sensual she thought she was drowning in pleasure. Burt had given her light kisses when he'd walked her to her cycle other Saturdays, but even that first kiss out in the front yard had nothing on this one. There was something about the dimly lit room, the softness of the leather couch, the feel of his body next to hers.

She opened her mouth at his urging, and the deeper kiss shot a delicious sexual ache down her body, starting her legs trembling. Her arms around his neck, Sandy scooted her body just enough against his so he had to move over her. She wanted to feel his body pressed hard against hers, knowing the pressure would assuage her arousal. Temporarily.

She wasn't quite sure how far she wanted to have this continue, but she trusted Burt not to rush her. He kissed her slowly, deeply, and she sighed between kisses, running her hands over his shoulders and back.

He was driving her crazy, leading her deeper and deeper into a world of heat and sensation. She shifted her legs, restless now, wanting to feel him more closely. He moved with her, and she felt him slide between her legs so she cradled his hips and felt his arousal hard against her own.

She had to touch him. She pushed his chest gently and he levered himself up, balancing his weight on his elbows. Quickly, intent only on satisfying her need, she unbuttoned his shirt, then ran her fingers lightly over the curly hair on his muscled chest.

She felt his muscles contract, looked up and saw the darkness of his eyes. Their gazes met, locked, then she felt a slow smile spread over her face.

"Happy?" he whispered.

"Yes." She slid the shirt down over his arms, then gripped his bare shoulders and urged him down again. "I think this is what I wanted all along."

He laughed softly, then she felt his breath tickle her ear. "I love your honesty, Sandy. The things that come out of your mouth—"

"Mmm," she agreed, catching his lips with a kiss.

She jumped when she felt his fingers at the hem of her shirt, and Burt stopped, broke the kiss and caught her eye.

"Oh." All her breath left her in a sigh. She closed her eyes and tilted her head back into the soft leather. "You're going to hate this, Burt."

"I think I already know what you're going to say." There was a smile in his voice, and she opened her eyes just a fraction.

He *was* smiling.

"Come on." He kissed her neck. "Just say it."

"There's a part of me that wants to, and there's a part of me that wants to stay where we are a little longer. Do you know what I mean?"

He nodded his head, then shifted his weight slightly so they were lying side by side. "I do. We haven't had much time alone, and here I am, rushing you to the finish line."

"I was rushing things, too."

He kissed the tip of her nose. "I want you to be happy, baby. Whatever you say, goes."

Something about the way he said baby melted her insides. It was strange how one man could use the endearment and make it sound ridiculous, while another could turn it into pure, vocal lovemaking.

"I guess I'd better go."

"I'll walk you out. And call me when you get home."

When Sandy stood, she was surprised to find herself leaning against Burt. Her legs seemed to refuse to obey her.

"You're one hell of a good kisser, Burt. You've knocked me off my feet."

"I don't think my kisses had anything to do with it." He held her firmly in the circle of his arms. "But the wine might."

Sandy glanced back at the coffee table and the half-empty wine bottle.

"It's not that much. I shouldn't even be feeling it."

"Sandy, I drank beer."

She stared at the bottle. "I drank all that?"

"So it wasn't my kisses after all."

She started to laugh, her cheek against his chest. "It's a good thing you're a nice guy."

"Sleep with me."

Slowly, she raised her head until their gazes met. "Is this a pass?" She bit her lip against the giggle that was bubbling inside her.

"I'm serious. No sex. Just sleep with me. I'm not in any shape to drive you home, either."

"Hmm." She smiled up at him, then blew a wisp of hair out of her eyes. "I'm thinking."

"I could be noble and put you in the guest room, but I'm not *that* nice a guy."

"Really sleep?"

"Whatever you say."

"The really crazy thing is, I believe you. Okay. Let's go."

"Stay right where you are."

He was laughing! Then she felt Burt's arms come around her waist. He lifted her over his shoulder, then started walking in the direction of the hall.

"Me Tarzan, you Jane." She couldn't resist, and as soon as the words were out of her mouth she started to laugh.

"I think you've got it backward, but as long as you don't call me Cheetah, there's hope."

She'd never been in Burt's bedroom. It was done completely in blues, a soothing, quiet room. He set her down on the king-size bed, on the royal blue down comforter. The only sound was the faint hum of the air conditioner.

"I'll get you a pair of my pajamas. If you want to take a shower or something, just say the word."

"This'll be like a slumber party, but even better, huh, Burt?" Sandy closed her eyes and dissolved into giggles. She wasn't drunk, but the situation suddenly struck her as hilarious.

She heard the pajamas hit the bedspread, and opened her eyes. Burt was looking down at her, his arms crossed. But there was an amused gleam in his eyes and she knew he wasn't mad at her.

"What about the boys?" she whispered, remembering that Ryan and Michael were merely down the hall.

"They're dead to the world when they're asleep. And there's a lock on the door. They respect it. I've never believed in children running through their parents' bedroom whenever they want to."

"You're sure?"

"I've locked the door. Don't worry about it."

"Are you mad?"

"No. I've kind of thought about you here."

"You have?"

"Yeah."

"Like this?"

He paused before he answered, and she detected a faint twitch at the corner of his mouth, the beginning of a smile. "Not exactly like this, no."

"How was it?"

"Don't you want that shower?"

"Do I smell like Wadsworth?"

"I didn't mean it that way. I thought it might relax you before you fell asleep."

"I think it might be a great idea. Some cold water sounds good right about now."

"Tell me about it."

She walked into the bathroom with as much dignity as she could muster, closing the door behind her. Slowly, her movements careful and controlled because of the slight fuzziness in her brain, she stripped off all her clothing and folded it into a neat pile beside the sink. She set her sneakers beside the small wastebasket.

Then she stared at the mirror, and her naked reflection. For one crazy moment, she considered waltzing back into Burt's bedroom, but then she turned toward the shower and stepped inside.

The stinging spray felt so good, sluicing over her skin. She found some shampoo and washed her hair, then took her time lathering the bar of spicy-scented soap over her skin.

When she heard the faint knock on the door, she called out softly, "Burt?"

The door opened. "Are you okay in there?"

"Just dandy."

He closed the door again, and she rinsed off quickly and turned off the shower. Stepping out onto the fluffy rug, she wound her hair into a towel, then reached for another and began to vigorously dry her body.

She still felt a little shaky. Lying down on the couch, she hadn't felt the amount of wine she had drunk. Once on her feet, she had. Now she felt better. A little.

She found the pajamas. They were huge. She discarded the bottoms, put on the top and pulled on her panties. Then she rubbed her hair dry and looked around for a comb. Nothing.

Sandy opened the door a crack. "Burt?" she whispered. "Could you do me a favor?"

"Sure."

"My purse—"

"I already brought it in. Here."

She found her comb and worked the tangles out of her hair. There was no blow dryer in the bathroom, so she hung up her towels and glanced in the mirror.

She was sure Burt had meant her to wear both the top and bottom of his pajamas. But the top came down to her thighs, and the pant legs would drag on the ground. Her mind made up, Sandy left the bottoms on top of the hamper, shut off the light and stepped into the bedroom.

Burt was lying in bed, just in jeans. He glanced up over the magazine he was reading as she walked up and slid beneath the comforter on the opposite side.

"It was a great shower," she said, never taking her eyes from his as she burrowed against the pillow.

"Sounds like a good idea." And he got up off the bed and headed toward the bathroom. She closed her eyes and listened to the sound of running water, but suddenly found she wasn't sleepy at all.

When he came back out, he was clad in a similar set of pajamas, both top and bottom.

"Oh, take off that top," she whispered. As his head jerked up, she realized what she had said and how it must have sounded.

"You know, Sandy, this might not have been such a good idea."

"I think it was excellent. Come on, Burt, we can be like those couples in those old movies. Besides, I like to look at you."

"Jesus." He started to unbutton the top, then shrugged it off his broad shoulders. "You're driving me crazy, Sandy. I'm not blaming you, but I think I might have been a little insane to think we could sleep in that bed and not—"

"We could always change our minds."

Now he was really staring at her. He sat down on the edge of the bed. "I don't want us to make love because you're feeling a little happy."

"I'm not feeling that happy. I mean, I'm not drunk, Burt. I was just thinking while I was in the shower. I've always believed in not putting things off. I always thought the best thing to do was just jump right in."

"Are you saying this because you think it's what I want to hear?"

"No, not at all." She sat up in bed and reached for his hand. "I was a little scared out on the couch because things were happening so fast. But—and I know this is going to sound ridiculous—taking that shower, I was thinking about us, and I really think we should.''

"I don't know, Sandy." He looked away from her, then suddenly glanced back and said, "What the hell am I doing? Any other guy would jump at the chance, and here I am trying to talk you out of it."

"I thought it was a little strange myself."

"There are some things we have to consider."

"There, I knew I was right! Don't you see, Burt, if we didn't feel close enough to each other, we wouldn't even be able to talk about things like this."

"Are you using anything?"

"No. But I bought some protection a week ago. It's in my purse."

"I did, too. It's in the night-table drawer."

"See? Our minds were on the same track." She smiled at him. "That wasn't too bad. Boy, now I'm not nervous about sleeping with you at all. If we can get through that, we can get through anything."

He lay down next to her and closed his eyes. "I'm exhausted. Maybe I could take a rain check."

She was about to protest when she saw one blue eye open, then wink.

"Maybe you're right, Burt." She played along, feeling her mischievous streak surfacing. "Perhaps we should start fresh, now that we're sure we're ready."

His move was sudden. He rolled quickly on top of her, his hands grabbing her wrists as he used his body to pin her against the mattress. Her eyes widened in understanding as she felt him against her.

"I'm about as fresh as I'll ever be," he said, his breath warm against her ear. She shuddered against him. "And I think—no, baby, I *know* we have a long night ahead of us."

Chapter Seven

"Boy, you older guys," Sandy said sleepily. "You know, there's something to be said for experienced men."

"Mmm?" Burt slid across the warm tangle of sheets and she felt his arm come around her waist, pulling her close against him.

He kissed her, and her mouth, relaxed and soft, yielded to the gentle pressure and opened. Morning light against the curtains turned the bedroom a soft, dark shade of blue. She could hear birds twittering outside.

Her fingers gripped Burt's shoulders tighter as the kiss deepened, grew more intense. She felt his body stir against hers, then he broke the kiss and buried his face against her shoulder.

"I can't believe the way you get me going," he said, then laughed softly, self-consciously. "It almost embarrasses me."

"No, no. I love it. I love—" She stopped. The words had almost slipped out, and now she was the one feeling self-conscious.

He raised his head, his face so close to hers she couldn't look away. "What were you going to say?" His blue eyes were narrowed. Intent.

"I love it. The way you make me feel—"

"No. What you were going to say."

She couldn't answer, could only stare at him. Though her instincts were screaming he cared, she couldn't face the thought of admitting how she felt and discovering he didn't feel the same way.

"I can't—"

"Say it." He kissed the corner of her mouth.

"No." But her lips trembled, and he caught the slight movement with another kiss.

"Come on, baby," he whispered. His lips moved against hers, caressing, persuasive. "Say it for me. What you were going to say."

"I—" She closed her eyes, and knew she was going to take that ultimate leap of faith. There was no other way.

"I love you."

He was silent. She opened her eyes, her chest tight, prepared to face the hurt. The look in his blue eyes did away with any doubts she could have had. They burned with pure joy.

"Say it again," he whispered.

She smiled, feeling total euphoria spread throughout her body. "I love you."

"Burt."

"I love you, Burt."

Later, he lay beside her on the bed and kissed her, touched her face, told her how much he loved her. They both fell asleep smiling, he with his arms tightly around her, his face against her hair, and she with her cheek pillowed against his chest, the steady beating of his heart the last thing she heard.

THE LOUD KNOCKING ON THE DOOR woke Burt out of his deep sleep. For a moment he was disoriented, but when he saw the small lump next to him beneath the comforter, memories of last night—and why he was tired—came back.

Not wanting Sandy to wake up, he eased the covers back and slid out of bed as gently as he could. He pulled on his pajama bottoms quickly and hopped to the door, fumbling with the fastening.

The bedroom door opened and, standing so he blocked the view of the bed, Burt looked down into Michael's face.

''Dad, Ryan's making himself breakfast and he has cereal and milk all over the place.''

''I'll be right out, Michael. Give me just a minute to pull on my jeans.'' He scratched his head sleepily. ''What time is it?''

''Almost nine. We're gonna be late.''

''I'll be right out.''

He closed the door, then glanced at Sandy as he reached for his clothes and dressed hurriedly. She was nestled snugly under the covers. He'd be back before she even woke up. Sometimes the gods worked in mysterious ways. Michael and Ryan were going to be spending the day with a neighboring family. The father, George, a kindhearted man Burt trusted implicitly, had agreed to take his three boys and Michael and Ryan to the zoo.

His original plan had been to spend some time with John Savage and his motley crew. But now he had better ideas.

"Burt?" Sandy's voice was sleepy.

"Stay right there. Don't go anywhere. I'll be back in half an hour." He gave her a quick kiss, a light pat on her fanny, then left the bedroom, closing the door firmly behind him.

THE SMELL OF FRESHLY BREWED COFFEE teased her nostrils. Sandy slowly opened her eyes and saw Burt smiling down at her. He had a Styrofoam cup of coffee in his hand, and there was another on the nightstand. In between them was a bag of Winchell's doughnuts.

"Hi," he said softly.

"Hi." She sat up slowly, then winced as her muscles protested.

"I plead guilty on all counts."

"It's not your fault." She pulled the covers around her shoulders, more for warmth than modesty, and leaned against his chest. Burt was wearing a faded pair of jeans, nothing else.

"Where are the boys?"

"I sent them away for the day. I told them, 'When your father gets this lucky, the two of you have to play at your friends' for the next three days.'"

"You're terrible. Where are they really?"

"George took them to the zoo." He handed her the other coffee.

"Who's George?" She took off the top and sniffed appreciatively, then took a careful sip. It was still hot.

"Saint George, patron saint of single fathers who desire a day alone with the woman they love."

She felt herself melting inside. "I thought I dreamed all that when I first woke up."

"No dream. Have a doughnut. There's a chocolate one in there somewhere."

She reached into the bag and pulled out the most disgusting, gooiest, calorie-laden doughnut in the bag. "Who's George?"

"George and Alice. I know it sounds like a sitcom, but they're two of the sweetest people on the block. They have three boys. The middle and youngest are Michael and Ryan's age. So we trade them back and forth. I took all the boys to Magic Mountain last month, so this month George is taking them to the zoo. Michael and Ryan love him."

"Did you plan all this?"

He feigned innocence so well she almost laughed out loud. "I swear to you, Sandy, I thought I was going to be stuck with John Savage today."

"You should be writing."

"No, I want to be with you."

"What do you want to do today?"

"Besides lick that chocolate off your chin?"

"Besides that."

"I thought we might take a shower together, then go out for brunch."

"We could have brunch right here. I could make us something."

"I don't want you to think—"

"—that the only place you want to be with me is in the bedroom. I won't think that, Burt. We were up all last night, so if there's no chance of Michael and Ryan coming home early, we could take a nap together—"

"—and then a shower—"

"—and then just kind of see what happens."

Burt finished his coffee and lay back down on the bed. "Somehow, I don't think I have to be psychic to figure out what's going to happen."

IT WAS A LAZY, wonderful Sunday. They slept in, made love, showered, made love, made brunch, took a nap together, then made love one more time before the boys were due home.

"I'm destroying your writing career," she teased him. They were both lying in bed, eyes glancing at the clock every so often. Michael and Ryan would be home within the hour.

"It's already destroyed," he replied.

His answer surprised her. "What do you mean?"

"Nothing."

"Are you having trouble with the book?"

He sighed. "I've been a little blocked. It's a strange feeling. It rarely happens."

She turned toward him. They were sharing a pillow, and she could see the tense line of his jaw. He'd been so relaxed only moments ago, and she regretted bringing up a subject that upset him. If they talked it out, it might help.

"Do you want to write this book?"

He was silent for such a long time she thought she might have hit a nerve he didn't want exposed. But he finally answered, and his words surprised her.

"No. No, I don't. I can't believe I never asked myself that question."

She took a deep breath and determined to plunge ahead. "Why are you writing it?"

"I never asked myself if I *wanted* to write it. I just told myself I had to. It's money in the bank. I want Michael and Ryan to be secure, and things have been...I had to buy out Anne's share of the house to keep them here, and it seemed like a good idea at the time. You know, the home they loved. Everything was changing, and I thought if I could keep just a little bit of their lives the same, it might not be as difficult an adjustment. But the guy she had who did the estimate—he was good. She wanted big bucks, and she got them."

He was quiet, and she waited, knowing there was more.

"I feel...like I'm in the middle of a midlife crisis or something. I think about changing my life completely, quitting the writing and working at something else. And I know that would be crazy, because I used to love to write. I don't know what the hell's the matter with me. This sounds so damn self-indulgent."

"No, it doesn't."

"Then I think, you'll probably wing through this like all the other idiots, with a blond bimbo and a sports car. Or maybe a motorcycle—" His chest stiffened beneath her hand, and Sandy knew he was realizing how she could interpret what he'd just said.

"Sandy, I—"

"No, I understand. Besides, *I'm* the one on the motorcycle."

"I don't know what I want. Just getting through the days has been the top priority for so long. I—I feel like I've kept everything in the back of my mind for so long. I haven't felt alive in a long time. Except last night. I felt alive with you.''

She caressed his bare chest gently, and he covered her hand with his fingers.

''I don't want to set such a lousy example for my children. It kills me to think they might grow up and see their father as a person who was afraid of life, who couldn't go out there and give it everything he had. But I've just been so tired, for so long.''

Burned out, Sandy thought. ''You're questioning things, Burt. That's brave in itself. There are a lot of people who go through life and don't even ask any questions.''

''And there are a lot of people who ask themselves all the questions and are gutless when it comes to finding the answers.''

''You're brave, Burt.'' Her voice was very soft. ''You took two little boys and tried to create a life for the three of you. You've been through a lot and you're tired. I know what that's like. And you're a good writer. I read the first three of your John Savage books, and you got me right into all that adventure.''

He hugged her tightly against him, turning so they were lying side by side in his bed.

''You have a real special way of making me feel good.'' He kissed her, his hand reaching up, his fingers tangling in her long hair. When he broke the kiss, he looked at her for a long moment, then said softly, ''Will you stick around for a while, Sandy?''

''As long as you want me. Now lie back—I have this terrific method of relieving tension.''

MICHAEL AND RYAN CAME HOME dusty, sunburned and content. When Burt met his sons and his neighbor at the door, both Michael and Ryan were looking up at him expectantly. George spoke up, explaining.

"We're going camping the week after next. Nothing special, just out by Alice's folks. If it's all right with you, I know my kids would love having yours along."

"Can we, Dad? Please?" Michael looked up at his father, his eyes beseeching.

It was so rare he asked for anything. In one way, Burt wanted to keep his children close to him. Sandy had made him forget Anne for a short time, yet what she might do was always in the back of his mind. But he couldn't let the same fears that seemed to be dominating his own life ruin his children's.

"I'd pick them up Friday afternoon and we'd be back on Sunday. It's a safe campsite, Burt, out around Idyllwild. I know you have that book to finish, and I thought—well, Alice and I both thought this might help."

"Thanks, George." He smiled down at Michael. "I think it'd be okay, and I appreciate your asking them."

"No problem. I'll have Alice call you before we leave. I'll see you." And Burt watched his friend walk off down the driveway. George had grown fatter over the years, his waistline expanding in direct proportion to the thinning hair on his head. He was one of the kindest men Burt had ever met, and one of the only people he trusted his sons with.

When he and Anne had moved into the house, Ryan had been a baby and Michael only five. Alice had been over as soon as she'd seen the van, bringing a casserole and offering to help unload boxes. She and Anne had become friends that afternoon, having five children in common and all the problems and joys of stay-at-home mothers.

Both George and Alice had been absolute rocks during the divorce. They had never really taken sides, never asked uncomfortable questions. The last, futile time he and Anne had tried to salvage the marriage, Alice had taken Michael and Ryan under her roof for several long weekends so that he and Anne might have some privacy. The boys had felt as secure there as they did in their own home, having grown up running in and out of both houses.

The only exception was when Burt had a deadline. Then Alice, in very subtle ways, directed most of the action over to her house. He liked her a lot. Alice was a short, slender woman with dark hair and eyes that took in everything. Her snappy, sparkling personality was in direct contrast to George's laid-back attitude. Even their looks contrasted. George had sandy hair and pale blue eyes. On the surface, they seemed total opposites, but something had worked over the years. The one thing Burt knew they had in common was a deep, abiding love for their three boys.

Closing the door, he listened as Ryan told him all about the koala bears and Michael explained exactly where the camping trip was going to be. They all retired to the den and he sat back on the couch, one son on either side, and enjoyed the moment intensely. They weren't fighting, they were both happy. Neither of them had that tight, worried look on their faces that he had grown to hate.

Ryan tired out first, right after his shower, and Burt tucked him into bed. Then he and Michael stayed up and watched a television program on space. Michael loved looking up at the sky, and Burt had bought him a telescope for his last birthday. His children were so different. Ryan was sturdier, his feet more solidly planted on the ground. He had adjusted much more quickly to the divorce, but then he had always been more his baby than Anne's.

Michael was a dreamer. A worrier. He had been his mother's pet, before she had decided husband and family were not what she wanted. He had believed— *still* believed, Burt corrected himself—his mother might come back. And in some ways he had grounds for his belief. Burt knew it must have seemed, in the first year, that he was waiting for Anne to come home. He worked in the house, and had rarely gone out except to shop for food and other necessities. And to do things with the boys. Nothing for himself. Those days still seemed vague, a dream period. The only thing he could remember clearly was the pain. And the day he woke up and realized the pain was gone,

He'd kept his social life separate, not wanting to confuse his children further. He'd brought two women home to meet them and had been surprised to find himself watching the way they acted with his children. Both had made it subtly clear that he was the one who interested them, not his sons.

That had changed things. It wasn't as if he was looking for a mother for his children, but he had found himself wondering how these women would ever fit into his life if they didn't even seem to particularly care for Ryan and Michael.

Sandy had been different. They still hadn't really gone out on what could be called a conventional date, yet she had managed to fit right in. Yes, Michael resented her, but Burt knew his older son was going to resent any woman who replaced his mother in his father's heart. He was afraid, and it would take time. But it could be worked out. Ryan had been won over from the first.

Burt leaned back on the couch, his eyes on Michael, lying on his stomach closer to the television screen.

He sometimes thought about when he had first fallen in love with Sandy. It was a strange thing, love. This next Saturday was Wadsworth's last lesson, so it had been only eight weeks since they met. He could remember the way he'd felt when he'd first seen her. There had been an instant attraction that had been closely followed by a strong sense of liking this easy, capable woman. He had found himself looking forward to Wadsworth's lessons.

That first afternoon by the pool he'd been supremely aware of her physically. He'd wanted to kiss her and he had. Phone conversations had followed, and he'd enjoyed talking with her. She'd never been boring, and they hadn't run out of things to talk about. Some of his dates had been horrifying, when he had realized they had exhausted their storehouse of subjects to discuss and had several hours left in each other's company. That had never happened talking with Sandy.

One of the last barriers had been breached when he had seen the way she handled Ryan, taking his upsets at being ignored and hurt by Michael and turning them into feeling good about helping Wadsworth learn his lessons. He was sure the last thing Sandy needed while she was training a dog was a five-year-old running all over the place and being a distracting influence. He had admired her calm, unflappable attitude.

He liked the way she genuinely liked children.

Burt was brought out of his thoughts by a burst of music that sounded suspiciously close to the theme from *Star Wars*. Michael was slowly getting to his feet, and Burt sat forward.

"I'm going to go to bed, Dad."

Then Michael surprised him. Ryan had always been his more openly affectionate child. Now Michael approached him and threw his arms briefly around his neck, hugging tight.

His arms came around the thin, wiry body and he hugged Michael to him, smelling shampoo, the smell of the laundry detergent they used, and his son's own distinct scent.

"Thanks for letting us go." Michael stepped back, and Burt felt his throat tighten at the glowing excitement on his son's face. "George says you can see all the stars up there at night really clear. Maybe sometime we could go up there, just you and me."

"Count on it." Burt stood up and walked with his son in the direction of his bedroom. "I'll let you go first, then you can show me everything you discovered."

He stood next to Michael's bed as his son got inside. He still tucked Ryan in, but Michael had made it quite clear he considered himself too old. But Burt still kissed his son good-night.

"'Night, Dad."

"Good night, Michael."

Back in his bedroom after his nightly check of the house, Burt lay in bed and stared at the ceiling.

They had survived. Survived some of the worst possible times a family could ever go through. He was deeply thankful to George and Alice for giving Michael and Ryan a sense that some families did indeed weather the storms and continue intact. For a long time he had felt so guilty that he had failed so many people. Anne. His children. His father. Even though Michael Thomson Sr. had died almost three years before his son's divorce, Burt still felt he had failed his father.

He closed his eyes, his head against the pillow. Then he smiled as Sandy's scent invaded his senses. It wasn't any particular perfume she wore, just a clean, fresh smell that belonged to her.

He missed her already. He'd started missing her when she had kissed him goodbye and walked to her motorcycle. He'd liked falling asleep next to her, seeing her first thing when he woke up. He liked the way she'd moved close to him, even in sleep. The feel of her cheek against his chest, her hair against his face, the sound of her heart beating when he'd laid his head against her breasts.

He glanced at the clock. Twenty after nine. Not too late. He picked up the receiver and dialed her number.

She answered on the third ring.

"Hello?" Her voice was low, thick with sleep.

"Did I wake you up?"

"No. No. Hang on, I'm going to prop up my pillows. I was just kind of half asleep, you know?"

Once she was back on the phone, he came straight to the point. "What are you doing the weekend after next?"

"Nothing, I think."

"Then I'd like you to spend it with me." Quickly, he outlined the camping trip and the privacy it would afford them.

"I'd love it."

This time he was sure he heard something else in her voice.

"Sandy, are you all right?"

"I'm fine. It's just—" She laughed briefly, self-consciously. "Every so often, I—I get bad cramps."

"Oh." There were some advantages to having been married, one of them being intimate knowledge of feminine physiology. "If I was there, I'd offer to rub your back."

"I'd take you up on it."

He settled back against his pillows. "A friend of mine once said that cramps were God's way of getting even with women for multiple orgasms."

"Ohhh." She lengthened the word, a knowing tone in her voice. "So it was time for me to pay in spades, right?"

He started to laugh. "If I'd known, I would have adjusted my behavior accordingly."

"Don't even think it. I loved everything about this weekend. I wouldn't have wanted to change one bit."

"I know what you mean." He closed his eyes. "I love you," he said, testing the words on his tongue. They were still so new, yet felt so right.

"I love you, too." She sounded tired.

"Do you take anything for it?" He was still concerned.

"Enough Advil to kill a horse. Every time I promise myself I'm going to get something prescription strength, then once it's over, I just go on my merry way. It's only about three times a year or so. I'll live."

"Call me tomorrow if you still feel bad. Ryan's in playschool and Michael will be at the Y for a while. I could come by for about an hour."

"You don't want to see me in this condition."

"I'd like to see you any way I could."

"John Savage isn't going to like this."

"John Savage," he said slowly, a teasing note to his voice, "would behave exactly the same way."

"You writers always have the last word, you know that?"

"Yep."

They both laughed, then Sandy said, "I'll be thinking about you each time I ache."

"I always wanted a woman in agony over me," he teased.

"Burt?"

"Yeah?"

"I don't know if I subscribe to your friend's particular theory, but if it's true—"

"Hmm?"

"It's worth it."

When he hung up the phone and turned off the light, he was smiling.

Chapter Eight

"Thanks, Fred." Sandy sat up in bed and took the bowl of hot chicken soup from her roommate's hands. "Next time you're feeling this bad, I'll make you homemade."

"Campbell's is fine. How're you feeling?" He patted her feet beneath the bedspread.

"Like a truck ran over me. I can't believe a little thing like this gets me down."

"Well, I subscribe to a friend of mine's theory, and since you weren't home the other night, I'd say it's pretty valid."

Sandy swallowed a spoonful of the hot broth. "I already know all about it." She almost laughed out loud at the mournful expression on Fred's face. He hated it when she beat him out of a punch line.

"You knew?"

She nodded her head. "A wise man told me."

"A wise guy."

"That, too."

She continued to spoon down her soup, surprised that Fred didn't bounce off her bed and hit the floor running. Tall and lanky, he was always going in a million different directions.

"Sandy," he said, pushing his longish hair out of his eyes, "can I ask you a question?"

"Sure."

"How do you think Elaine feels about me?"

She set her soup on the small, round table by her bed. This was far more interesting than any meal. She had watched, over the past few weeks, as Fred and Elaine had gone around and around in their discussions about love. One thing was perfectly clear—they had totally different opinions. Elaine was much more cautious than Fred. She made up pro and con lists, thought things out carefully, weighed each decision. Fred believed in total spontaneity, living life on the edge and making a relationship a collective form of total anarchy.

They were crazy about each other. It was like watching *Moonlighting* in the privacy of your own home, but there weren't as many reruns.

"I think," Sandy said carefully, "that the two of you are nuts about each other."

She knew she had hit dead center by the spots of high color that appeared on Fred's cheeks.

"Get out of here. Elaine? Me? It would never work."

"You're right. It'll never work if you don't tell her you love her."

Now she had his attention. "I can't do that. I mean, if I love her—and it's still a big if—what if she doesn't love me? I mean, I'm not that successful yet."

"You will be."

"Yeah, but the guys she goes out with—"

"She's miserable. You know that first night you two went to The Improv?"

He nodded his head.

"That was her big topic of conversation for weeks. This, from a woman who jets around Europe the way you and I go to Sav-on. Come on, Fred, she's crazy about you. I think she has been since college."

"But—"

"How come you guys never went out?"

"Well..." He put his head in his hands. "This is going to sound incredibly sexist."

"Try me."

"Elaine was a little—well, a little on the—"

"Fat."

"Fat," he agreed.

"So she's not fat now. What's the problem?"

"It took me a little time to get beyond Elaine my buddy, you know what I mean? And every time I think of that father of hers, and what he would think of me—for her, I mean—"

"Will you stop thinking of yourself in terms of what it is you do? Fred, you're one of the greatest guys I know! You make me laugh, you lend me money, you make a mean bowl of Campbell's Chicken and Stars—"

"Sandy, don't make a joke—"

"I'm not. You have everything going for you, but you have to put your heart on the line. Tell her you love her."

He was silent, sitting on the edge of her bed, and her heart went out to him.

"I'll be gone the weekend after next. All weekend."

"You really think she thinks about me that way?"

"I know it."

"Okay. This is it. Enough is enough. All those talks, all those arguments, everything's been leading up to this. You're right, Sandy, we can't go on like this. I'll tell her. The deed will get done that weekend."

"Fred?" She picked up her soup.

"Yeah?"

"If all else fails, get her drunk and carry her back to the guest house and ravish her."

"You think Elaine would go for that kind of stuff?"

"I think she'd love it."

SHE WAS HALF ASLEEP when there was a soft knock at the door.

"Sandy?" It was Fred.

"Hmm."

"Mr. Savage is here. He'd like to see you." Mr. Savage was Fred's nickname for Burt.

She slowly came awake, having just taken another aspirin. "Okay."

Then Burt walked into her bedroom.

He'd never been to her house before, and now she could see he was taking in the large room. One wall of the bedroom had enormous windows facing the view of the Los Angeles skyline. She'd hung a profusion of plants instead of curtains.

Her bed was an old brass antique Elaine had found in one of the storage rooms when she'd bought the mansion. Sandy had done her entire bedroom in white, with white scatter rugs, white eyelet bed-spread, white candles on her small bedside table, a white wicker chair. She loved light, and the bedroom was bright and airy.

"Hi, Burt." She sat up in bed, adjusting the pillows behind her. Then, looking at him again, she saw he had a bouquet of bright orange tiger lilies in his hand.

"They're beautiful! Oh, Burt, you didn't have to."

"I wanted you to have something pretty to look at, as long as you're confined to bed. Fred said he'd bring up a vase."

"I love lilies." Then their eyes met and she knew he was thinking of Cici. They started to laugh.

"She isn't really all that bad," Burt admitted as he sat down on the edge of her bed. "She came over the other evening with some muffins for the kids. Peanut butter with chocolate chips. They loved them."

"Were you ever aware she was after you?"

"Yeah. She used to hang around when I did yard work, and sometimes her hints were pretty broad."

"And you were never even tempted?"

"Get out of here."

Fred came in with the vase and gave it to Burt, who promptly filled it with water and unwrapped the lilies. He arranged them in the vase, then set it on the table by the bed.

"Do you need anything else, Sandy?" Fred asked as he picked up the empty soup bowl.

"Not now. I feel a lot better." As she spoke, she glanced at Burt and smiled.

"I'll leave you guys alone. Good meeting you, Burt."

"You too."

Once Fred left, Sandy stretched leisurely in bed. "I think I'm going to take you up on that back rub."

"Turn over."

She felt her oversize T-shirt eased gently up over her head, then his hands were on her back, fingers kneading, palms stroking. He had a sure touch, and she could feel the tension swiftly leaving her body.

Sandy was surprised she didn't feel the need to say anything, to keep up her end of any conversation. Her feelings for Burt were such a paradox: she was intensely aware of him, yet comfortable at the same time. It didn't seem possible that two such contradictory feelings could coexist in one relationship. But they did.

"I think I'm going to fall asleep."

"Go ahead."

She closed her eyes, his hands warm against her lower back.

WHEN SHE WOKE, the sun was low in the sky, her bedroom walls bathed in a soft pink glow. She loved sunsets. Her windows let in enough western light that she could see what colors were in the sky sometimes just by looking at her bedroom walls.

She stirred. Burt had certainly left by now. She turned her head slowly and looked straight into his eyes.

"You're still here."

"I talked to Alice before I left. She agreed to take Ryan home from playschool with her son and pick up Michael after his lesson."

"She sounds like a terrific woman."

"She is. I told her I needed a little time to myself. She's always understood."

Sandy glanced at the clock. "How long can you stay?"

"She said she'd make sure they ate supper. We have some time."

"Will you hold me just a little bit?"

He shifted closer and gently took her in his arms.

"I was thinking," Sandy said. "About Ryan."

"Yeah?"

"Would you mind if I got him a hamster?"

"No. Tell me why."

"I've been noticing he doesn't play with Wadsworth as much. He's more your dog, Burt, since you trained him. He stays in the studio with you when you write, so Ryan's kind of all alone. He loves animals, and he always tells me about Butch at playschool, so I thought it would be something he would really like."

"I think he'd love it. Do you think Ryan would be all right with a hamster? He tends to get overly excited about things."

"If I explained everything to him, I bet he could handle it."

"When did you want to bring it over?"

"I thought since Saturday was Wadsworth's last lesson, I'd stop at the pet store the same morning and pick it up."

"Okay. I'm taking Michael out that afternoon. He likes to fly his plane in the park. It's one of those with a remote control. Anne's coming to take him out to dinner in the evening, so I thought I'd spend some time alone with him in case he wants to talk. He's been a little better with Ryan lately. I'm sure he'll come around to accepting you in time."

"I hope so." She thought about putting her thoughts into words, hoping she wouldn't be opening old wounds too deeply. Then, remembering her twin's philosophy, she decided to try.

"Was Michael hit harder by the divorce?" She had long thought that Ryan had taken his parents' separation with much less trauma than his older brother.

He was silent for a short time, and she thought perhaps he didn't want to answer the question. Then she realized he was merely gathering his thoughts.

"Yes. Ryan was— When Anne discovered she was pregnant the second time, she wanted to have an abortion. I guess we both knew the marriage wasn't working. I told her if she just had the baby, I would take it from there. I had just started working at home, so when Ryan was born I put his crib in my studio and just kept typing."

"Did you know that much about babies?"

"I'd been a pretty active father with Michael. I knew how to change a diaper. But I was lucky; he was a good baby. Alice helped a lot. I used to go over there a couple of afternoons a week, and she'd fill in the gaps in my knowledge."

"And Michael?"

"Michael was in kindergarten when Ryan was born. I don't know if I could have handled both of them at home for long periods of time. I admire Alice in that respect. Her first two are only twenty-two months apart."

"Where was Anne?"

"She went back and stayed with her mother for a while. Then she went on a long vacation, to see friends on the East Coast. Her mother always believed she was selfish, but I'm not as sure. She was deeply depressed after Michael was born. I wanted her to get help. I'd accepted the fact that Michael was going to be our only child, then Ryan came along. I really don't think she could have gone through everything twice, raising another child. Knowing how depressed she was about Michael's birth, I felt sick about making her go through it all over again, but I couldn't bring myself to feel good about the alternative.

"So Ryan's used to coming to me. Not much has changed in his life because Anne was never really there for him. He loves her, but he doesn't need her the way Michael does. That's a little oversimplified, but it's the way it is."

"You must have loved her a lot." She remembered the pictures in the den, especially the expression on Burt's face in the wedding portrait. She didn't feel he still loved Anne, because he wasn't the sort of man who would tell one woman he was in love with her while still emotionally involved with another.

"I did. I can't remember one great moment when I stopped loving her. It was just an accumulation of things. I hated what happened to our children, but I'm not sure it could have turned out any other way. Betsy—Anne's mother—could never face the fact that something might be wrong with her daughter, so she simply believes Anne is cruel. The only thing I wish could have been different—I wish she had gone for help. I tried to get her to go, but she was her father's daughter, and her family solved their problems on their own.''

"Do you believe that? That people have to do it themselves?''

He was silent, collecting his thoughts. Her cheek was resting against his chest, and she could hear the steady beat of his heart.

''I think you have to decide you want to get better or solve the problem. But there's no shame in getting help. I know how overwhelming life can get, and there were times when if I hadn't had Jerry to talk to, I might have jumped off a building.''

"Who's Jerry?''

"A friend of mine. A therapist. He helped me straighten out a lot of my feelings. Anne and I were caught up in some pretty damaging patterns. I was going to be the perfect provider, the man who went out and conquered the world. She was going to be the perfect wife and mother. Neither of us was any good at it. She never should have gotten pregnant in the first place. I always felt responsible for that.''

''But you weren't totally responsible.''

"I should have known better. When I first met her, she was so...different. Wild. Exciting. I'd always been the good guy, the guy who did the right thing. There was this...feeling between us. I wasn't careful. We had to get married. Sometimes I wonder what might have happened if I'd taken better care of her.''

''I've never believed all women should be mothers,'' Sandy said.

''You would have been up against a solid rock wall trying to explain that to Anne's parents. Or my father. We had that in common. Our parents were convinced you did things a certain way, that men and women had their place. So Kent is miserable at work, wishing he was at home painting, and Betsy does more charity work than any five women and would have been brilliant in her husband's position."

"But things are changing, don't you think?"

"Not soon enough. My dad—he never knew me. *Really* knew me. When we were growing up, he could silence any of us with a look. He never had to lay a hand on us. But he used to make you feel like such a fool if you stepped off the path he'd laid out for you."

Her instincts working overtime, Sandy said, "He didn't like your being a writer, did he?"

"He never knew. If I had told him I wanted to write, it would have been the same as if I'd told him I was homosexual. Men who were really men didn't do that kind of stuff. My father was an All-American, a college football star. He sent me to a military high school, Sandy. He believed he was doing the best thing for me. My younger brother, Chris, had a nervous breakdown his senior year at the University of Michigan, right before he graduated. He didn't know how to hide his other side from Dad, and he didn't know what he was going to do with himself when he got out of school."

"Is he okay now?"

"He's surviving."

"Did you ever tell your father? About the writing?"

"I tried. At first. He kept saying, 'But what are you really going to do?' I couldn't make him understand it was the only thing I wanted to do."

"Did Anne believe in you?"

"Yeah, she did. She encouraged me to rebel, and I liked that. She used to flout her parents' values in their faces, but when push came to shove it was still a superficial rebellion. Yet in a lot of ways she wanted me to be happy. Sometimes I think it's why she left. But she still gets crazy."

"Do you talk to her?"

"She still calls."

"Has she remarried?"

"Yes. She's pregnant again. And not very happy."

They were silent for a time, watching the shadows lengthen in the bedroom. Then Sandy tilted her head back slightly so she could see his face. She touched his cheek with her fingertips.

"I didn't mean to bring back so many memories."

"I'm sorry. I didn't mean to talk away the entire afternoon."

"Don't feel like that, Burt. I love you."

"There are times I wonder why."

She eased herself up, balancing her weight on her elbows so she looked down at his face. She didn't feel at all self-conscious in only a pair of lace panties. He'd seen her in less.

"You're not a failure, Burt. You're just re-creating a lot of your life. Experimenting. Just the way you are with Michael and Ryan, you're not at all like your own father. And that's something, because those patterns are hard to break."

He reached out slowly, took a strand of her hair in his hands and slid it through his fingers.

"You really get to me. Physically. Emotionally, you always hit it straight on. That was one of the biggest fears in my life, that I'd bring up my kids just like Pop brought us up. I can remember holding Michael in the hospital and making a promise to him that I was going to try and be different.''

"You are."

"I used to wait for my father to come home at night. I just wanted to play catch. I'd wait and I'd wait, and I'd watch the sun get lower in the sky. If I was lucky, he made it home before sunset. We'd start to play but, Sandy, he just didn't have any patience. I'd start to laugh—I used to laugh just because I was happy—or I'd throw the ball a little wild, and he'd turn around and go inside.''

She could feel the tension in his body, so she leaned over and brushed her cheek against his. "I hear Ryan laugh all the time.''

He caught her up in his arms, pulling her so she lay across his chest, their legs tangled together.

"But, Michael. I look into his eyes, Sandy. It's always there, that fear. And every time I see him, the tightness around his face, that look, I remember exactly what it felt like. I see myself doing to him what Pop did to me. And I love him. I can't tell you how much I love him, and it tears me up to see that look in his eyes.''

His jaw was tense, his eyes suspiciously bright. Sandy leaned forward and kissed him.

"It's going to be all right. Come on, come over here.'' Slowly, carefully, she rolled over onto her back and held out her hands.

She embraced him when he moved into her arms, feeling as if her heart were breaking apart and flowing down her arms into her fingertips. She shifted, so his head rested against her breasts.

"I love you, Burt," she said quietly, and felt his arms tighten around her in silent response.

"How are you so smart, so young?" The question was barely a whisper.

She took a quick breath, then decided to let the words go before fear called them back.

"The next time we have together, ask me about Jimmy." The minute the words left her, she felt a sense of peace envelop her.

And she knew she loved him enough to let him know everything.

"SANDY, PLEASE can I open the box? Please? I think my hamster is lonely." Ryan's eyes were riveted on the small cardboard box on his bed.

"Hang on one second, just let me get the rest of the shavings in here." Sandy had taken pity on Burt and bought an enormous bag of red cedar shavings for Ryan's hamster. Though hamsters didn't smell if their cages were cleaned regularly, the cedar would further eliminate any odor.

"Okay. Now remember our deal. I'm going to lift him into the cage very carefully, and you can't make any loud noises and startle him. All right?"

Ryan nodded his head, looking as if he were ready to explode.

The small box was quivering slightly, and a scratching noise was coming from it. The hamster was trying to escape. Sandy sat down on the bed and carefully opened the box. Ryan sat on the other side, craning his neck to get a look at his pet.

"Oh!" It was all he said as Sandy carefully lifted out the black-and-white baby hamster. The little animal was terrified, and Sandy quickly stood up, then knelt by the cage and deposited him inside, shutting the mesh door and latching it firmly.

"There you are. Let's watch him get used to his cage."

Ryan was speechless. The reality of having his very own hamster live in his room was beginning to sink in. Sandy watched him out of the corner of her eye. He was fascinated with the little animal, and she suspected that a great deal of his day at the playschool was spent watching Butch.

"Look, Sandy, he's eating!"

The hamster had found the small bowl of food she had set out and now was busily stuffing its pouches with sunflower seeds.

"My teacher told me Butch likes to stuff his face," Ryan said.

"He stores his food inside his pouches. See how big the one side is?"

"Is he going to get hurt?"

"No, he knows when to stop."

"Can we watch him for a long time, Sandy?"

"As long as you want."

"Good."

While Ryan watched, she filled the water bottle and hooked it to the side of the cage, then swept up the cedar shavings that had fallen on the floor and put them in the cardboard box. After throwing the box away and storing the shavings and food on one of Ryan's toy shelves, she sat down next to Ryan on his bed.

"What are you going to name him?"

"Hambo. I wanted to call him Rambo, but Daddy said Hambo would be better."

Burt's sense of humor made her smile. He seemed to take it in stride that both his sons were obsessed with guns and war games. Ryan and Michael still played "Killer" with all the boys on the block. She hoped it was just a stage they were going through.

Now, as she and Ryan sat on the bed, her thoughts drifted back to this morning. She had given Wadsworth his last lesson, run him through all the basic commands she and Burt had spent eight weeks teaching him. Wadsworth was a happier dog; there was no doubt about it. He was easier to be around, and therefore received more attention from people. The funniest result was that he had come to adore Burt, and followed him around like an adoring slave.

They had all eaten lunch together. Burt had fixed hamburgers. She had been aware of Michael's resentment, and had been careful not to touch Burt or unconsciously do anything that might make Michael uncomfortable. She and Burt had told Ryan about the hamster the night before, and he had bounced all over his seat, excitedly telling his older brother that he and Sandy were going to go to the pet shop and pick out his very own pet. She'd thought of just swinging by that morning, then realized Ryan would probably have as much fun at the pet shop as he would with the hamster.

So Burt and Michael had headed for the park, and she and Ryan, in one of Elaine's cars, had gone to pick up Hambo. She had thought Ryan would want to look at all the tanks full of tropical fish, snakes, lizards and turtles, but aside from a quick stop at a giant cage full of baby rabbits, he had headed straight for the hamsters.

Hambo had been asleep in his food bowl, and it had been love at first sight.

She had taken Ryan to one of the largest pet shops in Los Angeles, on the corner of Beverly and Crescent Heights, so the drive there and back to Sherman Oaks had taken some time. Elaine's M.G. was a fun car to drive, and she had zipped the little sports car up over Laurel Canyon and into the city. Ryan had loved the ride, telling her it was more fun than Magic Mountain.

Ryan was right up against the cage watching Hambo. Each time the hamster did anything, whether it was eat a seed, drink from the water bottle or dig through the shavings, Ryan called her attention to it. She had made him promise to leave the animal in the cage for at least a day to settle in. She had also bought a plastic exercise ball, and planned to show Burt how to coax the hamster into it and snap it shut.

Sandy was so entranced with watching Ryan watch Hambo that she didn't see Michael leaning in the doorway until he spoke.

"That's Hambo?"

Ryan looked up. "Come and see him, Michael! He takes a drink out of here, and Sandy said he'll get on the wheel, too!"

"I can see him from here."

Sandy sat very still on Ryan's bed. She didn't like Michael's attitude, but felt it wasn't her place to say anything. Their relationship was still too precarious.

"My mom's coming over tonight," he informed her, his hands in his jeans pockets. He was watching her.

"That should be great. What are you going to do?" Burt had told her Anne was going to take Michael out to dinner, but she wondered if he would offer the information.

"She's taking me out. Just me."

Ryan was so engrossed in watching Hambo groom himself, he didn't hear his older brother.

"That should be a lot of fun."

"Are you going to be here?" His tone told her what he thought of that.

She had decided from the beginning she would be nothing but honest with him. "I think we're going to rent a couple of movies."

He stared at her, then said quietly, "She's a lot prettier than you are." Then he turned abruptly and left the room.

Sandy knelt down on the floor so she was closer to the hamster cage. She was glad Ryan hadn't paid any attention to the interchange. Michael's words hadn't hurt her. She knew Anne was prettier, in a purely classical way. And she knew Michael was hurt by her presence in his father's house. Every time he saw her, all it meant to him was that his mother wasn't with them.

"He combs his hair with his paws, Sandy."

"He sure does. We'll watch him until we go to the video store, then we should let him get a little sleep."

"Will he stay up all night like you said?"

"Yes."

"I'm going to watch him."

She couldn't help but smile. Ryan would be fast asleep long before Hambo had finished his nocturnal wanderings.

"Let's go find your dad and see what movies he wants to rent."

LATER IN THE AFTERNOON Sandy took her motorcycle and went down to the video store. Burt had given her his card, and she rented the titles they had come up with: *Raiders of the Lost Ark*—she was a Harrison Ford fan and Ryan would like it; *The Purple Rose of Cairo*—Burt was a Woody Allen fan, and they could watch it after Ryan pooped out; and *The Adventures of Robin Hood*—the Disney cartoon was Ryan's absolute favorite in the world.

Heading back toward Burt's house, Sandy wondered if she really wanted to meet Anne. She knew Burt wasn't masterminding the evening for his masculine ego. They had decided to rent some movies several nights ago so Ryan could have a special evening, too. And Burt wanted to be home when Michael returned, to make sure all had gone well.

As she turned into the driveway, she determined to make the best of the evening. She felt secure in Burt's love, and that was all that mattered. And to be perfectly honest, she had wondered what Anne was like. A picture could tell you only so much.

They finished supper early, a pepperoni pizza and a salad, while Michael was getting ready in his room. Sandy had cleared off the table and was busy distracting Ryan from going in and checking on Hambo. The poor animal had had an exhausting day, traveling from West Hollywood to Sherman Oaks, from a cage with his brothers and sisters to a small, energetic boy's room.

If she were a hamster and saw Ryan watching her, she'd be a little scared. She knew Ryan meant well and would do nothing to deliberately hurt his new pet, but he was so excited, it wouldn't hurt to let the hamster have some time to settle in.

She looked up when Michael came in the kitchen. He looked absolutely beautiful in his dark blue suit, light shirt and tie.

"You want some ice cream before you go, Michael?" Ryan asked hopefully, and Sandy knew he was hinting they should have some dessert.

"Nope. I'm eating with Mom."

"What time will she be here?" Sandy asked, wondering if she would ever break through the emotional wall Burt's older son had put up between them.

"Six."

Twenty minutes.

"Maybe we could give Hambo some ice cream," Ryan suggested.

"Hamsters don't eat ice cream. Little boys do."

He smiled at her. Ryan certainly knew how to turn on the charm.

"I don't think your dad would mind too much if I made us both ice-cream cones." Anything to keep busy.

"I'll get the ice cream." Ryan got off his chair, then began to drag it across the kitchen to the refrigerator.

AT 6:20 MICHAEL WAS SITTING stiffly on the living room couch. Burt, Sandy and Ryan were in the den, Burt explaining for easily the tenth time why Hambo was tired from moving across town and would probably not want to play in his exercise ball.

Sandy noticed that Burt kept his eye on the clock. It seemed time was passing at a torturously slow pace. She kept glancing toward the living room, where she could just see Michael's profile if she craned her neck.

At 6:40 Michael walked into the den.

"Dad, call her. Maybe something happened." His face was tight, his eyes anxious. And Sandy remembered what Burt had told her about feeling scared all the time he was growing up.

She glanced up at Burt questioningly when he came back into the den.

"No answer." He pulled out his billfold. "Sandy, will you do something for me?" His voice was pitched low, and she knew he didn't want either of his sons to hear.

She didn't hesitate. "Sure."

"Take Ryan and go down to the shopping center at Ventura and Van Nuys. I think there's a cartoon playing at one of the theaters. Here are the keys to my car."

She didn't question his idea, nor complain about the fact that their evening had been disrupted. Burt had to know what he was doing.

"We'll leave right now." She raised her voice slightly. "Hey, Ryan, want to go for a ride with me?"

"Can Hambo come?"

"Honey, Hambo's tired out from riding in the car." She glanced at Burt. "I thought we might get some candy." She hated using sweets as a distraction, but the longer they stayed in the den discussing their evening out, the more tense she knew Michael would become.

"Okay. I'll get my sweatshirt."

"I'll get your sweatshirt," Sandy said quickly. Once Ryan went back into his bedroom, she wouldn't be able to pry him loose with a crowbar. She was painfully aware of Michael, sitting quietly on the sofa in his suit, as she crossed the living room to the hall.

Within minutes she was backing Burt's station wagon down the driveway and wondering if Anne was going to come and take her son out to dinner after all.

ONCE SANDY AND RYAN WERE GONE, Burt took a sheaf of manuscript pages and a pencil and moved into the living room. He sat in a large, overstuffed chair directly across from Michael and turned on the lamp next to him.

He pretended to correct pages, making a pencil mark in the margin from time to time. But his true attention and concern were focused on his son.

Michael simply sat, until the clock on the mantel softly struck seven. Then he got up and walked toward the hallway, heading for his room.

As soon as he left the room, Burt set the manuscript down on the table next to his chair, then sat forward, his hands clasped between his knees.

He knew Michael would want some time. He was an extremely sensitive boy and if he was crying, the last thing he would want would be for his father to see him. At the same time, Burt ached to go in and comfort him. One of the hardest lessons he had ever learned as a parent was that you simply couldn't shield your children from pain. The world had plenty of it to give out and didn't discriminate between children and adults.

When he heard the sound of glass breaking, he jumped to his feet and ran lightly down the hallway.

"Michael?" He stuck his head in the door of his son's room.

"I'm fine, Dad."

"Do you want to talk?"

"No."

"I'd like to sit with you for a while."

No answer.

Burt picked his way through the littered floor, arriving at the side of the bed at last. He sat down next to Michael and as he covertly scanned the room he saw the broken glass, and exactly what had shattered.

The ceramic picture frame had been thrown against the wall hard enough to break it. Tiny shards of glass sparkled faintly on the corner of the hardwood floor.

The picture had been ripped cleanly in half, his smiling face on one side, Anne's on the other. Michael's had been torn.

He had to look away.

Michael was silent for such a long time, there were several moments when Burt tried to think of something to say. But he couldn't.

Then, finally, his voice flat, Michael spoke.

"She's never coming back."

Burt closed his eyes. Raising his children was the biggest challenge he had ever faced, infinitely more challenging than trying to make a plot fall into place. They asked you so many questions about the world, and why it was the way it was. He didn't understand it himself, so how could he possibly explain it to them?

Tonight he could only give his son total honesty. Because if he hoped for something that was never going to happen, it would destroy him. What was it Jerry had once said? "Hope can kill you." He hadn't understood it at the time. He understood it now.

"No."

"Why did she leave?"

"We had problems, Michael. It had nothing to do with you."

He was silent for a short time, then said, "Why didn't she come to see me tonight?"

He felt so old, as if someone had beaten on his body for a long time.

"I don't know."

Michael was turned slightly away from him on the bed, and Burt watched as his thin shoulders shifted beneath the suit jacket.

"Why doesn't she love me anymore?" His voice cracked on the last word, and Burt watched as Michael's body stiffened, ever so slightly. Just enough so he wouldn't cry.

It was like stepping back in time and seeing himself all over again. Michael might have inherited Anne's physical traits, but he possessed his father's emotional control.

"She does love you. As much as she can. Michael, I don't know what I have to do to make you believe it, but it's true."

"Do you still love her?"

Instinctively, he shied away from hurting his son, but knew the truth was kinder than living in illusion.

"No. Not the same way."

"Do you love Sandy?"

He could give Michael nothing but his best.

"Yes."

"Okay."

Okay. Like he's talking about what we're going to watch on television. Michael, let it out. It won't destroy you. That only happens if you keep it inside.

He waited. Watched.

"I'm okay now, Dad. You can go."

"I thought we'd just sit here for a while." He knew all the signs, he'd held in his share of feelings. "A man doesn't cry," Pop had told him. His father had believed it, and it had killed him.

Now he watched as his son covered his face with his hands, his back still turned in the hope his father wouldn't see him. The stiff set of his shoulders was softening. Trembling.

The first sniff was loud in the quiet room.

"Michael." He laid his hand on his son's shoulders, and was surprised when he turned and threw himself against his chest, arms tight around his waist.

"Oh, Michael." He leaned against the wall so he could hold his son securely, wishing all the while he could keep the pain at bay.

The front of his shirt was wet before he heard the whispered words.

"Oh, Daddy."

He closed his eyes and wept with his son.

Chapter Nine

Sandy and Ryan made it to the theater with fifteen minutes to spare before the next showing of Walt Disney's *Dumbo*. Ryan, ecstatic with his good fortune—a hamster and the movies all in one day—danced around Sandy's legs as she paid for the tickets, bought a tub of popcorn and a medium cherry coke. She entertained Ryan by answering his questions about Hambo until the cartoon started.

She had brought plenty of napkins with them for the popcorn, knowing Ryan was an absolute genius when it came to making messes out of food. But she was glad she had the napkins when the cartoon reached the scene where Dumbo's mother was jailed and reached between the bars to rock her baby in her trunk.

Sandy usually cried whenever she saw this scene. Her twin, Jimmy, had always teased her about it. This time, she burst into tears.

They kept running down her face long after the scene was over. She swiped at her cheeks with several napkins and blew her nose as quietly as possible. Ryan was mesmerized by the cartoon. His eyes never left the screen.

Afterward they stopped at a little café that served *gelato*, and she treated Ryan to a dish. She only half listened as he talked about Dumbo and his magic feather as she glanced at her watch.

It was almost nine. After Ryan finished his *gelato*, they would have to go home. She shouldn't have even kept him out this late.

Whatever Burt had wanted to do, she hoped he'd done it.

Her instincts told her Anne had never shown. If anything could be assured of destroying Michael, this would be it. Burt had probably wanted time with his son for precisely this reason.

"Want some?" Ryan slid the dish of chocolate *gelato* toward her. The entire bottom half of his face, from nose to chin, was covered with the Italian ice.

"You know, Ryan, you could take some tips from Hambo about eating," she teased as she reached into her bag for one of the napkins from the theater.

"I could stuff my face with ice cream!"

"I don't think so. Why don't you finish up and we'll go home."

As she turned the car slowly into the driveway, she saw Burt step outside the front door. Ryan had fallen asleep during the ride home, so when the station wagon came to a complete stop, Burt opened the passenger side door, unbuckled Ryan's seat belt and lifted him into his arms. Sandy locked up the car and followed him into the house, keys in hand.

She waited for him in the living room. Her gaze kept returning to the couch. She could almost see Michael sitting there in his suit.

When Burt returned, she handed him the keys.

"You must be tired. I'm going to head on home."

"No, wait. Stay just for a while. I'll make us some coffee."

They sat at the kitchen table, Wadsworth asleep at their feet. The house sounded strangely silent without Michael and Ryan awake.

She didn't want to ask, so she waited for Burt to volunteer.

"Anne never arrived."

"Oh, Burt. That must have been horrible for Michael."

"As strange as this may seem, I think it was good for him. He's been running away from the truth and keeping all his feelings bottled up inside. Tonight everything came out. There was no way to excuse what Anne did. He had to face up to the fact that she's not coming back."

Though his words could have been interpreted as uncaring, she could see the strain in his face, the slight redness in his eyes. He had felt every emotion Michael had been through in the way only a parent could.

"Where is he now?"

"Asleep. He's exhausted. He'll be up tomorrow, though. He's a resilient kid; he amazes me."

"I'm sorry you both had to go through it."

"I am, too."

They sipped their coffee in silence for a while, just listening to the sounds a house makes at night. Wadsworth sighing as he lay on the floor. The dry, summer wind making the bushes scrape against the house. The tick of the clock above the stove.

When she finished her coffee, Sandy washed her cup and set it on the dish drain. Then she walked back over to Burt, who had finished his coffee and was leaning against the refrigerator, watching her.

"Well, Ryan liked Dumbo."

"Dumbo and Hambo. You can't beat a combination like that." Burt smiled a slow, tired smile as he looked down at her. "I appreciate your taking Ryan for the day and getting him that hamster."

"I loved doing it for him."

"I feel sorry for that hamster. He'll probably love it to death."

"No, Burt, Ryan understands. I think pets are great for children. And your son's such an animal lover, I think he'll be fine. Just get on him right away if he disturbs Hambo during the day when he's sleeping."

He put his arms around her waist and pulled her slowly against him.

"Michael asked me about you."

"What?"

"He asked me if I loved you. I told him the truth."

"I hate to make him any unhappier than he already is."

"He has to understand that your being here has nothing to do with Anne being gone. Michael has a sharp mind. I think he already knows. But he has to feel it, too. I think some of it happened tonight."

She didn't say anything, simply rested her cheek on his shirtfront.

"He liked you a lot in the beginning. Until that afternoon by the pool."

"I know. I saw the look in his eyes. I don't want to cause any trouble."

"I don't think of it as trouble. It's more a settling-in period. He can get pretty smart-mouthed when he feels cornered, or he'll take it out on Ryan. But if you can just hang in and remember he's hurting."

"I'll do my best." Sandy tried, but she couldn't stifle her yawn. "I've got to get home."

"Stay with me. Just to sleep. This time it's a promise." His eyes held hers, his gaze warm and steady. "I'd just like to have you next to me tonight."

She stepped back and, taking his hand, walked with him toward his bedroom.

SHE WAS SLOWLY COMING OUT of a dream, and Burt was talking to her.

"Yes, he was hurt. How did you think he'd feel?"

She tried to form an answer, but she was too tired, so she simply rolled over. The movement jostled her further awake, and she realized Burt was talking on the phone.

"You could have called. You could have called and said something to him. Anything. Or at least made up some damn story. Anne, you can't keep blowing in and out of his life and expect him to be anything but confused. You're pulling Michael apart and I can't stand by and let you do that."

Anne. She moved her legs, slid to the edge of the bed. His shirt had fallen over the side, so she reached for it, slipped into it as she stood, then walked quietly into the bathroom.

Inside, she turned on the water faucet to drown out the slight sound of Burt's low voice, then sat down on the floor with her back against the wall. The bathroom was a little chilly after the warmth of the big bed, and she wrapped her hands around her shoulders, then rubbed her upper arms.

Her head was tilted back against the wall and she was almost asleep again when Burt opened the door.

"Sandy."

She opened her eyes blearily and held out her hand. He pulled her to her feet, then put his arm around her shoulders and walked her back to bed.

Once they were inside, he slid his shirt off her shoulders, then put his arms around her. He was so warm, and she moved closer.

"I didn't want to hear," she whispered.

"I'm sorry I woke you up."

"No, it's okay."

He was running his hand slowly up and down the length of her back, pushing her tousled hair aside so he could touch her bare skin.

She sighed and moved closer, knowing what he was asking. In answer, she touched his shoulder, then his cheek, then lifted her face. The bedroom was dark, and she kissed his jaw, then he turned his head ever so slightly and their lips met.

He kissed her slowly, one hand in her hair, the other caressing her back. They stayed that way for a long time, until he softly cupped her breast and she broke the kiss, her breath expelled on a long, slow sigh.

She tried to touch him, run her hand over his chest, but he took hold of her fingers with his other hand and extended his arm slightly, preventing her from touching him.

"This is for you," he whispered. "Just relax."

He made love to her slowly, kissing his way down her breasts and belly, touching and kissing her intimately, making her want him so badly her entire body ached to feel him inside her.

Yet even when they came together, he controlled their rhythm, imprisoning her hips tightly with his hands, slowing his strokes so she hovered just on the edge of release.

"Please," she whispered, her body twisting feverishly beneath his.

He covered her mouth with his own, but kept them suspended in sensation.

She bit his lip gently, and when he raised his head, she whispered, "Now, Burt."

He gave her what she wanted, and pleasure washed over her in shattering waves so intense her body shook. She arched against him, wanting to be as close as possible. But when she finally lay quietly beneath him, breathing deeply, he was still above her, inside her, arousing her.

When she opened her eyes and looked up into his face, she managed a weak smile. Her eyes were used to the darkness now, and she could see his answering grin.

"If that theory of yours is really true, I'm going to have to pay for this."

His breath tickled her ear. "I lied." His eyes softened. "I love you, Sandy. Every time we're in bed together, I try to make sure you know it's true."

"I do. I love you, too." Her hand smoothed down his back to his hard, muscular buttocks. "This time I get to use my hands, or else I'm not playing."

He laughed, then sucked in his breath when she touched him.

"That's cheating," he whispered.

"That's getting you crazy."

She was still laughing when he started to kiss her.

"MICHAEL, WHY is he doing that?" Ryan said.

Sandy glanced at Burt and tried to stifle her grin. Ryan was driving his older brother crazy, asking him questions in the middle of *Crossroads*, one of the movies they'd rented. Michael liked guitar playing, so Burt had made sure to pick out at least one movie of the three that would appeal to his son. Sandy had brought over her popcorn popper, so she, Burt and the boys were sitting in the den Wednesday night, watching movies.

"Because he has to beat the devil. Be quiet, Ryan, this is my favorite part!"

For a few minutes there was total silence, except for the movie, then Ryan said, "Michael, why did he say that?"

"Dad, get him to shut up!" There was no real nastiness in Michael's voice, just the typical frustration of an older brother.

"But we can do it backward," Ryan said, meaning they could rewind the video. "Michael, why did—"

"Dad, I'm going to kill him!"

"Ryan, come up here." Burt patted the couch he was lying on. The boy got up off the floor where he had been sitting next to Michael, and lay down on top of his father.

"Daddy," he whispered, touching Burt's face. Burt opened his eyes. "Why did he—"

Sandy stood up and took one of the empty pop-corn bowls into the kitchen. She loved watching Burt with his kids. Earlier that evening, she had helped Ryan coax Hambo into his plastic exercise ball, and she and Burt had laughed over Wadsworth's incredulous expression as he'd come around the corner and seen the hamster scuttling along inside the ball.

Michael had come home in time to watch videos and had decided to join them, especially when he found out one of the movies was his favorite.

He hadn't said anything to her, but he hadn't given her any of his particular looks or made any remarks. And Sandy found herself hoping, for everyone's sake, that she and Michael could learn to coexist peacefully. She wasn't really sure if she ever expected Michael to like her, but she hoped he would give them a chance to get to know each other better.

She'd baked brownies—from a mix—while Hambo had rolled around on the floor, and now she cut them into squares and placed them on one of the plates Burt had set out on the counter. She set the knife down inside the baking pan, then picked up the plate and carried it back into the den. Setting the brownies down on the coffee table, she then lay back on the couch that was perpendicular to the one Burt was lying on. She didn't feel comfortable lying around with Burt in front of his children, especially since she knew Michael was still sensitive about her being in their home at all.

Michael had rewound the solo at the end, but he must have smelled the brownies because he turned around and took one off the plate.

You're being ridiculous, she thought as she watched him take a bite, chew it, then swallow. He took another. At least he wasn't gagging.

She reached for one herself, along with a napkin, then lay back on the sofa, wondering if he would say anything at all.

When Michael reached for a second brownie, he glanced back at his father.

"Dad, you should have one of these. They're pretty good."

Sandy smiled, recognizing praise for what it was. Michael's attention was on the screen, but as she glanced at Burt, Ryan sprawled on top of him and fast asleep, he winked at her.

BURT LEANED BACK in his office chair and surveyed the stack of manuscript pages that were beginning to pile up on the table next to his printer.

Wadsworth was stretched out at the side of his chair. It was the damnedest thing, but the dog rarely left his side. Ever since their training sessions, the sheepdog had decided that he belonged to Burt after all. Ryan had Hambo and Wadsworth had Burt.

He could rarely go anywhere around the house or yard without Wadsworth following loyally at his side. The dog adored him. Thank God he had established some house rules early and made sure Wadsworth slept in the kitchen.

He felt good. The book was coming along. He had almost two-thirds of it done, and he was sure he would make his deadline. John Savage would come out on the stands once again, ready to do battle with the forces of evil in a cruel, unkind world.

But there was something different about this book. He was finishing it up, and doing some of his best work, but he felt as if he were saying goodbye to Savage.

Or the man who started out writing those books.

It was the strangest feeling. He had no idea what he wanted to write or where he wanted to springboard to in his career, but he was happier than he'd been in a long time.

The day after Michael's breakdown Burt had felt terribly tired, but he'd entered his studio and begun to write with something that resembled his old rhythm. His mind had seemed sharper, his word choices clearer. John and his female partner, Sheba, worked side by side, dedicated to destroying the black-hearted scum of the earth.

It was almost noon before he understood. He was no longer emotionally attached to John Savage, or to the ways he did things.

The genre he wrote in was clearly defined. Men were men and men were tough. Only the strongest survived, and Savage was certainly a prime specimen of machismo. But Burt had always tried to dig a little deeper, pull out the more interesting facets of his behavior.

He had learned so much writing the Savage series. Twenty-three books later, how many more things could one larger-than-life fictional hero do?

And then there had been the dream. He'd been talking in his sleep, then shouting. Sandy had woken him, scared the noises might frighten the boys.

Lying in bed with her, he had told her the dream.

"I was standing next to Savage, watching him talk to Michael. He was pointing out the difference between two different types of machine guns, and telling him how they worked. I kept trying to talk to Michael, to get him to come with me, but he couldn't hear me. Then I tried to grab him, but it was like this wall of Plexiglas was between us. I couldn't get to him. And then I started yelling at him to jump through the wall and come with me."

"Do you believe in dreams being tied in to your subconscious?" she asked.

"I'm sure they are, but damned if I know what this means. I'm probably just overdosing on the guy. I mean, I wish I could write about John just the way he is, with all his faults and everything. I hate having to stick to this—this *thing*! It's so hard to have any sort of emotions toward a man who's more a machine than a human being."

"I know what you mean." She looked so soft and vulnerable tucked beneath the down quilt on his bed. "That's what I like the best about watching *Magnum P.I.* Tom Selleck could have played that guy like a macho brute. But he gave him a little humor, made him a little self-deprecating. I was hooked."

"But I don't know why Michael was there. Other than he was on my mind because of last night."

"Do you want to hear what I think?" she asked.

"I'd love to."

She snuggled up against him, her head close to his on the pillow. "I think you're fighting against the idea of a man being a machine, like—I feel nervous saying this, Burt—like the worst aspects of your father. And you don't want Michael to be hurt by that way of thinking and acting, so you're trying to do it differently with your life and his. And John Savage gets thrown in there because I think you might have been drawn to him in the first place in order to work out some of your feelings."

He knew he was staring at her as if she had sprouted two heads.

"I think you may be right."

"But, Burt, I've read six of your books now, and you may not believe it, but Savage gets better and better. You've rounded out his character. You gave him a sense of humor and you made him unafraid to work with and trust a woman."

"I can't see it. Some days I'm just so tired of the whole thing."

"Burt." She eased herself up on her elbows and looked down at him, then kissed his cheek. "I know you've been really frustrated. But maybe you could ease some of that by thinking about another direction. There's nothing that says you can't continue the Savage series and write about something else."

"I have no idea what, though."

She was looking at him so intently he finally said, "Say it."

"I don't want to be butting into your career."

"But I like your instincts."

She looked down at his chest, and when the words came out, they were very soft. "I think you should write about your father."

He lay very still.

"About what it was like, growing up that way. About what you felt inside."

"I've always thought that kind of writing was nothing but pure self-indulgence."

"Maybe. It might be a bridge to what you eventually want to write. You don't have to publish it. If you're worried about money, you could write it and still continue with the Savage series. But, Burt, what if one man read what you wrote and could identify with it? Wouldn't you feel wonderful about reaching someone that way?"

"I suppose I could work on it in my spare time."

"There's no such thing as spare time."

He turned his head and looked at her intently as the softest blush rose in her cheeks. "Where did that come from?"

Her eyes were very bright. "Jimmy."

He remembered the conversation they had had in her bed that day, and how she had asked him to ask her about Jimmy. The following week had been hectic, and it had completely slipped out of his mind.

Now he wanted to know.

"Tell me about Jimmy. Who is he?"

"My twin brother."

He was astounded she had never brought him up before this. "You have a twin?"

"I did. He died the spring we turned twenty-two."

"Sandy, why didn't you tell me this before?" All thoughts of his dream were completely forgotten.

"I don't talk about Jimmy with that many people. I mean, I do with people who knew him, but I've never really explained to anyone what he meant to me."

He touched her face. "Tell me."

"He saved my life."

Burt was positive there were tears in her eyes. He enfolded her in his arms, her cheek against his chest. "Baby, tell me."

He'd almost found out about Jimmy before Michael knocked at the door and said Ryan was trying to let Hambo out of his cage. Burt had raced down the hall and found a tearful Ryan trying unsuccessfully to latch the cage door. He had wanted to pet him and hadn't been able to secure the cage shut.

Then, once Michael and Ryan were up, there was no more time to talk.

He was fairly certain the boys didn't know Sandy spent many nights with him. She had taken to parking her motorcycle behind the carport by the garbage so they couldn't see it. He was careful about locking the master bedroom door, and usually Sandy waited until he and the boys left before she got up and dressed and went back home. He had given her a set of keys shortly after their first night together.

Now he leaned forward, staring at the bright green letters against the gray background. He saved his work, cleared the screen and took the disc out. Then he inserted a blank disc, already formatted, into the second disc drive. He placed his hands on the keyboard and faced the blank screen.

Nothing came to his mind.

He stared at the screen, his stomach tight, trying to remember what Sandy had said that morning.

About what it was like growing up that way. About what you felt inside.

His fingers began to move, slowly.

Scared. So scared. All the time. I can never remember anything else.

His typing was slow, his heart was in his mouth, but the screen began to fill with the familiar green letters.

He was connected again.

BURT WAS DRYING the last of the lunch dishes and thinking about the weekend when he heard a familiar voice float up from the driveway.

"Sandy is my friend."

He smiled. Ryan sounded sure of himself, and that was good.

"She doesn't like you, she likes your dad. That's what I think."

He stopped drying the dish in midsentence, then tried very hard to place the voice. He wasn't positive, but he thought it was one of the kids down the block. Carrot-red hair and freckles came to mind, but he still wasn't sure.

"She bought me a hamster," Ryan said.

"So what? She stays overnight with your dad, that's what my mom said. I bet she's *his* friend, not yours."

Burt was about to set the dish down and go outside when he heard another voice.

"Shut up, Kevin." Michael.

"She's *my* friend," Ryan said. "She's going to my school with me, and she puts Hambo in the ball—"

Then Burt heard Kevin use a very explicit word with deliberate cruelty.

Burt set the dish down the same instant he heard the scuffling begin. He slammed out the back door and around the side of the house to the driveway. Michael was on the concrete with a red-haired boy. They rolled down the sloped drive, and before Burt reached them Michael began pounding the boy with his fists.

Ryan stood to the side, wide-eyed.

"Hey! That's enough!" Burt grabbed Michael beneath his arms and pulled him off Kevin, who sat up and glared, holding his hand over his bloody nose.

"It's true," Kevin yelled. "You know it's true."

"Get out of here," Michael screamed, his wiry body taut with fury as he fought against Burt's hold, "or I'll bust your head open!"

Burt kept a tight hold on his son as Kevin scrambled to his feet and let himself out the gate. Only when the boy rounded the drive and disappeared around Cici's cypress trees did Burt loosen his grip.

Michael wouldn't look at him.

"Daddy, is Sandy my friend or yours?"

"Shut up, Ryan!" Michael's temper flared again before Burt could respond to his young son.

He could feel Michael's body trembling beneath his hands.

"Michael, calm down. Let's get inside and put something on this scrape."

But his son twisted out of his grasp, then turned and faced him. "Is it true, Dad?"

He couldn't look away from the accusing expression on Michael's face.

"Does she stay here?"

He knew Michael wanted it to be a lie.

"Yes."

Ryan had come over and grabbed hold of his hand, and now Burt watched as Michael darted away and ran around the side of the house. He heard the slam of the screen door and knew Michael was retreating to his room.

"Daddy, why is Michael mad?"

He knelt down and put his hand on Ryan's shoulder. "He's mad about a lot of things, Ryan. Why don't we go inside and cut up a carrot for Hambo?"

"Okay."

And as Burt walked toward the back door, Ryan's hand trustingly in his, he wondered if growing up ever got easier at any age.

Chapter Ten

He left Michael alone for almost fifteen minutes, then knocked on his bedroom door.

"Go away, Dad."

"Let me take a look at your arm, then I'll leave you alone."

The scrape looked ugly under the light of the bathroom. It wasn't anything that warranted stitches, but it had to be cleaned and bandaged.

Burt took his time, knowing Michael would eventually want to talk, and hoping it would happen before he shut him out again.

He decided to try for a beginning.

"That was some fight. You must have been really angry with Kevin."

"He's an ass."

Burt finished swabbing the scrape, then began to look through the assortment of bandages in the first-aid kit. "Do you want to tell me about it?"

Silence.

"Michael, you can ask me anything. I'll tell you the truth."

He thought Michael was going to remain silent, but then the first question came out.

"Why does she stay here?"

"Because I ask her to."

"Why?"

"When you love someone, you want to be close to them."

"She's here during the day."

He knew what his son was getting at.

"Close in a different way."

"Why did you hide it? Were you ashamed?"

He'd taught his son so well.

"It's something very private, Michael. Between Sandy and me. I would have sat down and talked with you about it eventually. Maybe I was wrong not to do that right away. I knew you were unhappy about your mother. I just didn't want to make you feel worse."

He finished bandaging Michael's arm, hoping the conversation wasn't over. Burt was sitting on the edge of the bathtub, and he made no move to get up and leave.

"What Kevin said—" Michael repeated the last thing Kevin had said before the fight, the particular word. "Is that what you do to her?"

"No. It's an ugly word, and it has nothing to do with what I feel for Sandy."

"How come Kevin's mom knew?"

"She was looking for it. You know how if you look hard enough, you can find something bad in almost anything?"

He nodded his head.

"I think that's what she was looking for. A lot of unhappy people look only for the bad."

"Kevin's parents fight. I was there once. John and I went over to get him, and they were fighting. How come you and Mom never fought?"

"We did fight. We just did it when you weren't around. Sometimes I wonder if that was the right thing to do."

"I hated hearing it from him."

"I know. I'm sorry you found out that way."

"I guess I won't be going camping, right?"

"Why not?"

He looked genuinely puzzled.

"Michael, you know how I feel about fighting. But I was in the kitchen and I heard some of what Kevin said. He was trying to get you to fight. You think you started the fight when you jumped on him, but he started the fight by getting to you. I know you didn't deliberately go outside today wanting to get into a fight. There's a difference."

"So Ryan and I can still go camping this weekend?"

"Yeah."

"Will Sandy be here?"

He nodded his head. "Does that bother you?"

"Sometimes. When I think about Mom. But she got married to that guy, so I guess she's not lonely." Burt could see the new thought working itself through his brain. "Were you lonely, Dad?"

He thought his answer through carefully. "I guess I didn't know how lonely I was until I met Sandy. What I feel for her has nothing to do with my love for you and Ryan. But I also need time with her."

"I know. Like I like to be with my friends a lot."

He couldn't help smiling. "It's not exactly the same thing. But it's close enough for now." He cleared his throat. "I want things to be different for us, Michael. When I was growing up, I was scared to ask my Dad a lot of things. I don't want you to feel that way. I want you to come to me and ask me questions. It might be a little difficult, but I know it'll be easier than being scared."

"Okay."

"Don't get your information from Kevin. Ask me."

"I will, Dad." Michael started to smile. Burt had always loved his smile as a child, the way the expression slowly crept over his face until it reached his eyes.

"It felt kind of good, hitting Kevin."

"I bet it did. But I want you to remember something for me."

"What?"

"Almost all of the time, a real man walks away from a fight."

"Would you have, Dad? I mean, if Kevin had been a man and said those things to you?"

"No." He reached over and ruffled Michael's hair. "You got me there."

IT WAS LATE AT NIGHT. Sandy was in her bed, propped up against several pillows and wrapped in her white comforter. Panda was asleep on the rug. The house was quiet. Elaine and Fred were out together on another platonic date, and she was talking to Burt on the phone.

He'd told her about Michael's fight, about what Kevin had said to him, about their talk in the bathroom.

"That's one of the things I used to love the best about my own dad," she said, cradling the phone against her ear. "I never got the feeling he knew all the answers, or was this guy we had to look up to or be scared of. I always just liked him. I mean, he was my dad and I respected him, but he didn't try to act like he knew it all."

"How did your family get through Jimmy's death?" There was a tentativeness to his voice, and she wanted to put him at ease. She wasn't scared to talk about death. In a funny kind of way, she wasn't even afraid of dying, since Jimmy had shown her how to live.

"It was so hard. It was like my entire family was blown apart and no one fit into their places anymore. Everyone had to become someone else; we all had to come back together and look at each other in a totally different way."

"I think I know what you mean."

"It hit my dad the hardest. There were times he'd go out in the yard and I knew he'd be crying. My mother dealt with it by working all the time. At the end, Jimmy asked to come home, so she and I took care of him. That's what got her through, I think."

"What got you through?"

She didn't even have to think through her answer. "Jimmy. I know it sounds crazy, him helping me when he was dying, but that's the way it happened. I don't know, Burt, so many things have to happen the way they happen, I don't even question it anymore."

"You said once that he saved your life. I want you to tell me about that this weekend."

"I'd like that."

"Sometimes I feel like you know me so well, and I don't know as much about you."

"Maybe I like being a woman of mystery."

"No, I'm serious. I want to know things about you, Sandy."

"You will. I'll talk your ear off." She settled back snugly against her pillows. "Tell me about Michael and Ryan getting ready for their camping trip."

She could hear the smile in his voice. "Michael keeps telling me about seeing all the stars and Ryan wants to take Hambo along. I'm worried he's going to try and sneak him out of the house."

"Tell him Hambo likes his cage, and he'd be really scared out in the open. Make sure he understands that hamsters like to stay in their nests."

"That sounds good. He's asked me at least six times to make sure I remember to feed him."

"Tell him Hambo will put seeds in his pouch and store them so he can eat while he's gone."

"He's worried the hamster will miss him."

"Let him know we'll put him in the exercise ball every day, and pet him before we put him back in the cage."

"I'm glad you're coming over this weekend."

"So am I. Point out Kevin's mom's window and I'll wave at her as I walk in the door."

He started to laugh.

"Does Michael know I'm spending the weekend?"

"He asked. I told him."

"You're sure it's okay?"

"Yeah. He's a lot more aware than I give him credit for. He really floored me when he asked if I'd been lonely. They're so different, Ryan asking questions a mile a minute and Michael so quiet. But when he's ready to talk, it all comes out.''

''Reminds me of someone I know.''

He laughed again.

She told him about the dog she was training tomorrow morning; he told her about what John Savage had done that day. Their conversation wound down naturally, and Sandy felt herself growing sleepy.

''What can I bring tomorrow?'' she asked.

''Just yourself.''

''I thought I could make some cookies or something—''

''We'll go to the store on Saturday. Don't even think about bringing anything.''

''I know I'm crazy about you when even the thought of going grocery shopping appeals to me.''

''I'm just crazy about you.''

She laughed.

''I love you, baby. Be careful on that bike tomorrow.''

''Get in an accident before this weekend? Not a chance!'' Her voice softened. ''I love you, Burt. I'm counting the hours.''

''Me too.''

''Be sure to tell Michael and Ryan I hope they have a good time.''

''I will.''

''I'll be over at seven.''

''I'll be waiting.''

BURT LAY BACK IN BED after he hung up the phone. He couldn't stop smiling. It was going to be a great weekend for everyone. Michael and Ryan were so excited that he had barely been able to get them to bed. Even now, Michael was probably still awake, though he was sure Ryan had dropped off.

He had never had the luxury of spending two nights and days in a row with Sandy, and he was looking forward to it. Friday they would just relax. Saturday, he thought they might take a picnic to the beach if the weather was clear. And Saturday night he had made reservations at the Seventh Street Bistro on Seventh Avenue downtown. It was a tiny, intimate French restaurant Jerry had recommended, and from the sound of it he knew Sandy would love it.

He wanted to make the evening special. Romantic. He and Alice had once talked about how men asked women to marry them, and both of them had agreed that their respective proposals had left a lot to be desired. Burt had simply assumed, once he knew Anne was pregnant, that they would marry. Alice had told him George had said something brilliant along the lines of, "Well, we're spending so much time together now, we might as well."

"A woman wants to be romanced, Burt. George has been a terrific husband and father, but there's a little part of me that always wished he'd been just the teensiest bit romantic."

He remembered that conversation now. Alice had told Anne she envied her. In the early years of their marriage, when Burt had come home from the office, he had sometimes seen Anne was ready to snap. So he'd called Alice, asked her to look after Michael, then taken Anne for a long drive, just the two of them. They'd always stopped somewhere to eat, and never been gone longer than a couple of hours. He'd sensed her desire to get out of the house, away from their son, and feel free for just a little while.

Now he lay in bed and thought about Sandy, about how she would like to be proposed to. She was right; he was a lot like Michael, keeping so much inside. He always tried to let her know how much he loved her when they were in bed together, but he knew from experience that a woman needed more. And he wanted to make Saturday night something they would remember for the rest of their life together.

He glanced at the clock. Though he'd talked with Alice this afternoon, finalizing plans for the boys' camping trip, she wouldn't mind another call. Alice would still be up. She was a night owl, not really functional until around ten in the morning, and even then she needed a few cups of coffee to get her going. George loved the morning, threw back the covers at dawn and walked straight into the shower. Alice had told him more than once that there were times she hated his early morning cheerfulness.

But the house was hers late at night. Alice was a voracious reader, and once George and her three boys were asleep, she made herself a pot of coffee and picked up her latest paperback.

She'd still be awake.

He dialed her number quickly, and she answered on the first ring.

"Hello?"

"Alice? Am I calling at a bad time?"

"No. I'm disappointed in this book. The story sags in the middle, you know what I mean?"

"I do. I just finished a book you'd like. It was a series of essays about people in film. Cinematographers, editors, special effects, that sort of thing. I'll drop it by."

"It sounds fabulous. Let me tell you, I'm ready to leave everything behind and enjoy this weekend. You should come with us sometime, Burt. I know you like the desert."

"I was kind of calling about this weekend."

"Ah, you have plans of your own." She laughed, a low, delighted sound. "I have to tell you, Burt, your exploits have been the talk of the block. I don't usually stoop to listening in—unless it's really interesting—but a lot of women in the neighborhood were wondering when you were going to start seeing someone seriously."

"Are you kidding?"

"Burt, you remember those days, trapped in the house. What else was there to do? Ah, but I forget, you wrote."

"Alice, one of these days I'm going to break into your house, steal one of your stories and send it out."

"I would never forgive you—unless it got published."

He and Alice had talked a lot about writing when their children were young. She was an excellent writer, but still hadn't summoned up the necessary courage to send her work out.

"But this time," Alice continued, "I think the girls are getting the idea it's serious. And I have to say, everyone likes the idea of you with a young blonde on a motorcycle better than with Cecilia Forrest."

"Cici was never in the running."

"She thought she was. Have the muffins slowed down?"

"Yeah, they have."

"She's getting the message. So, what did you want to talk to me about?"

"You remember that conversation we had about marriage proposals?"

Dead silence greeted him from the other end of the line.

"Now, I don't want to hear about this conversation from anyone else on the block."

"Oh, Burt! I'm so happy for you. I've only seen Sandy from a distance, but she's darling. Ryan told me all about the hamster she bought him. Do the boys like her?"

"Ryan does. It's going to take time with Michael."

"He'll come around. I thought something might be going on. You were kind of secretive. So this is it. When do you plan on asking her?"

"Saturday night."

"Are you taking her out?"

"I've made reservations at the Seventh Street Bistro."

"Perfect. While you're there I want you to think of me, chewing on George's special hamburgers."

He laughed. George was a totally inept cook, who burned the outside of a hamburger and left the inside raw.

"I'll take you there if you send a story out. You don't even have to sell it."

"I might get over my fear for that. So, you're taking Sandy out—"

"I just want it to be something she'll remember."

"I've got something you'll think is really corny, but it's classy and romantic."

"Go ahead."

"Remember Robert Wagner and Natalie Wood? When they got married the second time—I mean, when he decided to ask her—he took her out to dinner and ordered the most expensive champagne in the place. Then, when she wasn't looking..." Quickly Alice outlined how the star had proposed to the woman he loved. "You do have a ring, don't you?"

"I bought it Monday."

"Oh, Burt, I envy her. I love George, but this is such a special time for both of you."

"I'd like you to meet her. I know you two will get along."

"Anyone who could get that dog under control has my respect. So, how do you like my idea?"

"I think it has definite possibilities."

"You'll let me know how everything turns out?"

"The minute you get back."

"I'll be thinking of you. Have you heard from Anne?"

"Not since she phoned last Saturday."

"I don't like it, Burt. She's too quiet. I remember when she was pregnant with Ryan, she always went deep inside and got real quiet before she got crazy."

He had confided his fears to Alice about Anne possibly trying to regain custody of the boys. She had taken him seriously, having known Anne for years.

"They should stay with you, Burt. They're happy. They were both over here the other day playing that horrible war game, and I was watching them out the window and thinking you did a good job, getting them through everything."

"Thanks. That means a lot, Alice, coming from you."

"I heard Michael got in a fight this morning."

"The grapevine's at work again."

"Kevin's going through a tough time. I think his parents are headed for a divorce. He was over here the other day and he didn't look happy. I'm sure whatever happened wasn't Michael's fault."

"We talked it out."

"Well, you'd better get some sleep. You've got a big day tomorrow. George and I will be picking up the boys around two. We want to get an early start against the weekend traffic."

"They'll be ready."

"I'm happy for you, Burt. You deserve it."

"Thanks. And I appreciate the advice."

"You would have thought of something."

SANDY WAS SORTING THROUGH her clothes and packing a small bag made of parachute cloth when Elaine knocked on the door.

"Come in."

"Take the blue cotton sweater. It makes your eyes look terrific."

She laughed. "I tell you what. Help me go through this pile, then we can talk. I'm just too nervous."

"I thought you felt comfortable with Burt."

"I do. But he still makes me nervous."

"I know the feeling. Take that top, forget the cotton dress and make sure you take those white pants. You won't need much more than casual stuff. But take one drop-dead dress. What about that mauve one, the strapless one?"

"I don't think we're going out anyplace that fancy."

"Take it. He might want to surprise you, and you don't want to have to come all the way back here. Don't forget panty hose and shoes. Do you need any jewelry? You can borrow anything of mine."

"No, I think that about does it."

"Then I can give you your present. This time it's from London."

"Elaine—"

"Close your eyes and hold out your hand. This is kind of for Burt, too."

Sandy did as she was told and felt Elaine set a medium-sized box in her outstretched palms. It was light.

When she opened her eyes and looked down, she saw a silver box wrapped in an electric blue bow.

"Well, open it."

She slid the bow off carefully, took off the lid, parted the tissue paper and lifted up the most exquisite teddy she had ever seen. It was the palest peach silk, trimmed with lace.

"Elaine—"

"Try it on."

Within minutes, she stepped out of her bathroom.

"I love it. This I'm definitely taking along."

"Just make sure to tell the Big B I considered him when I picked out your present. It's from one of my favorite stores in London."

"Thank you so much. Now I'm not as nervous."

"He'll take one look at that and his blood pressure'll go right through the roof."

"He's not that old!"

She changed her clothing, slipped the teddy inside her bag, then sat down on her bed next to Elaine.

"What's up? You seem a little depressed."

"You're going to think this is really stupid."

Sandy smiled, remembering Fred. "I don't think so."

Elaine fell back onto her bed with a sigh. "I'm crazy about him, and he doesn't even know I exist!"

Sandy stretched out on the bed next to her friend. "Fred?"

"Am I being that obvious?"

"No. But I can see it in both of you."

"Both of us? Do you think Fred cares for me?"

She nodded her head.

"Then how come he won't make any moves? We go out all the time and have so much fun, but at the end of the evening he simply says good-night and walks over to his house. I don't get it. Sandy, do you think I intimidate him?"

"I think he's scared."

"Scared? Of me? I've known Fred since freshman year. We were in the same English class."

"But he's in love with you. I mean, you're in love with him and that scares you, doesn't it?"

Elaine closed her eyes and nodded her head. "I'm so afraid I'm reading too much into this and I'm going to make a complete ass of myself."

"I know. Remember I said I felt nervous? When you love someone so much, it's scary. None of us is used to being opened up like that. It's easier to just go along and not feel so much."

"What should I do?"

"Maybe make the first move."

"How?"

"Well—" Sandy couldn't resist a smile. "What would be the equivalent of that black bathing suit? It certainly got things rolling for me."

Elaine's eyes widened. "We're going out to The Comedy Store tonight. I could wear that red sweater and my black leather pants."

"And that perfume he likes."

"And boots. You're right. I've been pulling on my jeans and old sweaters. I keep thinking we're still in college."

"And if worse comes to worst," Sandy said, hoping she would be forgiven, "get him drunk, lure him to your bed and ravish him."

"You think Fred would go for that kind of stuff?"

"I think he'd love it."

Elaine sat up on the bed, her eyes bright. "You're right! What's that expression you're always telling me?"

"There's no such thing as spare time."

"It's true. If I want to get something going with Fred, I'll have to take things into my own hands. What time are you due at Burt's?"

"Seven."

"If I can get us appointments at my salon, are you up for a manicure and pedicure? This guy I met in London said the major difference between American and European women was that European women wore prettier underwear and took care of their hands and feet."

"How can I refuse a challenge like that?" Sandy knew Michael and Ryan were leaving at two in the afternoon, but she had decided to come by later in the evening to give Burt time to relax and perhaps get some writing done.

"I'll make us an appointment and be right back."

When Elaine left, Sandy walked over to the far wall and sat down in one of the large windows. She glanced down at the manicured grounds below, the turquoise-blue pool and the small guest house beyond. The soft, flower-scented breeze caressed her skin, and she watched as the wind ruffled the top of the pomegranate tree in the garden.

"It always works, Jimmy."

"FEED HAMBO, DADDY!"

"He's got food in his pouches, Ryan. Now you make sure to do what George and Alice tell you."

"Bye, Dad." Michael's arms came around Burt in a swift hug.

"Have a good time, Michael. I want to hear all about the stars. And keep an eye on your brother for me, all right?"

"I'll watch him, Dad."

They had walked over to George and Alice's house, and were standing in the driveway as the camper was being loaded with last-minute necessities.

"Hey, you guys, come here! I want to show you where we get to sleep!" John, George and Alice's middle son, beckoned to Michael and Ryan from the door of the camper.

"You can go now, Dad." This was from Michael.

"Okay. Be good." He started to back away, feeling strangely adrift, when a familiar voice stopped him.

"What did you tell my wife last night? She's been walking around the house all day with the goofiest grin on her face." George, his arms heavily laden with sleeping bags, came down the driveway toward the camper.

"George, don't start with him!" Alice was right behind, carrying blankets and pillows.

"I put the kids' sleeping bags in the camper," Burt said quickly, not wanting George to trip over them.

"Good. We're almost ready to go. I don't know why we always have to do everything the last minute, but I guess it wouldn't be a typical trip if we didn't."

"Daddy."

Burt looked up. Ryan waved at him through one of the camper windows.

"Don't forget to—"

"Feed Hambo, I know."

"Alice, do we have everything? If we wait much longer, the traffic will be impossible."

"Honey, we're all set." She gave Burt a quick wink. "I envy you," she said under her breath. "Champagne, nights of passion... I'll be wiping noses and cleaning up after carsick kids."

"You're making me feel guilty."

"The only time I want you to feel guilty is when you think of me eating those hamburgers."

"Alice, I'm locking the front door. Did you lock the back?"

"Yes, honey." She stood on her tiptoes and gave Burt a quick kiss on his cheek, then said, "I want a full report when I get back. Well, not a full report, maybe a censored version."

He couldn't help but smile. "I'll check the house on Saturday and feed the cat."

"She'll appreciate it. Don't touch the fish. We have an automatic feeder."

"Ryan can call me if he gets homesick."

"I'll keep him busy."

"Are you guys going to stand in the driveway and gab, or are we taking a trip?" George's teasing was good-humored.

"We're taking a trip!" screamed Chris, his youngest, from the window.

"Bye, Daddy!" Ryan called.

Burt watched George carefully back the camper out the driveway. Alice was in the passenger seat, opening a pamphlet. He laughed. George's idea of a good time was to park the camper and relax. Alice always wanted to see all the local attractions. Burt had listened to Alice's version of their vacations many times, and knew that eventually they would compromise.

He waved until the camper rounded a bend in the road, then walked slowly back toward the house.

He'd always wanted to go camping with Anne, do things as a family. But as the years had gone by, it had been painfully apparent she wanted to distance herself from her family. He had always wondered if the depression she had experienced both during and after her pregnancies had destroyed any joy motherhood could have held for her. Sometimes, lying in the dark, he had envied George his marriage to Alice. She had sailed through her three pregnancies, giving birth easily, loving her children in a breezy and spontaneous manner. There had always been plenty of laughter in the Crowley household. Everything was blessedly normal.

He let himself in the front door, then surveyed the silent house. Wadsworth was barking outside, but aside from that slight noise, all was quiet.

Burt had fixed lunch for the boys and eaten with them, so he wasn't hungry. He thought of working on the book, but decided what he really wanted more than anything else was a short nap.

He had barely fallen asleep when the phone rang. He picked up on the second ring, rolled over on his back and placed the receiver next to his ear.

"Burt?"

Anne.

"Hi, Anne."

No answer.

"Anne? Are you there?" He waited just a little longer before asking, "What's wrong?"

He sat up on the edge of the bed. Seconds ago he'd been pleasantly relaxed, but now he felt adrenaline surge through him, as if he were getting ready to fight.

"I've been thinking about this for a long time."

He closed his eyes, willing her not to say it.

"I think children should be with their mother."

"Anne, no. Don't do this."

Again, it was as if she hadn't even heard him.

"I want my babies back."

Chapter Eleven

When Sandy parked her motorcycle in Burt's driveway, it was still light out. She and Elaine had spent an uproarious time at the salon, with each trying to top the other thinking up inventive ways to seduce Fred. They had even had Mary, the manicurist, laughing so hard she could barely hold the nail polish applicator steady.

Now, her fingernails painted Passion Flower Pink and her toenails sporting Wicked Fuchsia, Sandy secured the lock on her motorcycle, then pulled the parachute-cloth bag out of one of the storage compartments.

The house seemed strangely quiet. She knew both Ryan and Michael had already left on their camping trip, but usually Wadsworth was running around in the yard, barking. Maybe Burt had taken the sheepdog for a walk.

Hoisting the handle of her bag over her shoulder, she started up the brick walk.

When she reached the door, she knocked. Even though Burt had given her a set of keys, she didn't feel right about letting herself into his home if he was there. She waited, then knocked again.

Nothing.

There was a distinct possibility he could be in his studio, finishing up his novel. Sandy stood on the front step, wondering if Kevin's mother was parting her curtains at this exact moment and making some comment. She had been disturbed by Michael's fight. It was a tough balance, trying to have a relationship with a man who had children. She wasn't a fool, and didn't expect either of Burt's children to warm up to her instantly. Ryan had, but even that might change if she and Burt were to become even closer.

Not wanting to cause any further trouble, she stepped down off the front steps, then walked around the side of the house and unlocked the gate that led to the fenced backyard.

Usually Wadsworth bounded up to greet her. Burt had to be out walking him. As Sandy walked toward the back door, she wondered why he'd gone out of the house when he was expecting her.

The back door was unlocked and she let herself into the kitchen quietly. Sandy looked up as Wadsworth came slowly into the kitchen and stood looking up at her.

It had to be her overactive imagination. The dog had the most mournful expression on his face. His eyes, partially hidden by the thick hair, seemed so very sad.

"What'sa matter, boy?" She set her weekend bag and purse down on one of the kitchen chairs and knelt down, then scratched the dog's head. "Did Burt go out and leave you all alone?"

Wadsworth simply turned around and left the kitchen, walking slowly.

She wondered if he was sick. Usually he was bounding around, barking with pleasure if anyone besides the family came into the Thomson home. She still wasn't such a familiar figure that she didn't rate a few barks.

Something was wrong.

Suddenly scared, Sandy followed Wadsworth as the large dog headed for the den. When she stepped inside the room, her hand flew to her mouth and she stopped in the doorway.

Someone had broken in.

There was only one lamp turned on, but it gave off enough light so she could see the damage done to the room. The glass bookshelf, built in to the far wall, had been completely smashed. All the pictures that had been so carefully arranged were now lying in scattered disarray on the carpeted floor. Someone had taken the pillows off one of the sofas and thrown them all over the room, along with the cushions. An oil painting on one wall hung askew. The heavy glass coffee table had been upended, everything on it scattered across the plush carpet.

Someone had completely trashed the room.

But the television was still there. The VCR. And the stereo.

Where was Burt? Had he been injured?

She stepped farther into the room, and as soon as she walked past the sofa facing away from the doorway, she saw him.

He was lying on his stomach, his head pillowed on one arm, the other limp and hanging to the floor. Lying very still.

"Burt? Burt!" She was beside him in an instant, Wadsworth at her side whining.

His heart was still beating, he was breathing. She was about to panic when he rolled to his side and opened his eyes.

"Sandy." He closed his eyes and let his head sink back against the black leather. "I'm sorry."

"What's wrong?" *I'm sorry?* Her glance darted around the room again. Had he done this?

She leaned down so her face was close to his. "Burt, what happened?"

This time he rolled over on his back, slowly, as if every muscle in his body ached. Sandy moved closer, touched his cheek, smoothed the thick hair back from his forehead. "Please tell me what happened." Then a horrible thought struck. "Is it Michael? Or Ryan? Did something happen—"

"No. They're fine. For now." His voice was raspy, as if his throat were raw.

"For now?" She took his hand in hers and held it tightly.

"Anne called."

She was silent, thinking furiously. What could Burt's ex-wife have done to upset him so deeply?

He opened his eyes and looked at her. They were red rimmed and dull. Then he glanced away from her face and focused on the far wall, beyond her head.

"She's decided she wants to be a mother again."

"Oh, no," she whispered.

"She told me she's going to fight for custody. Now that she has her life back together. A new husband she can't stand, a baby she doesn't want on the way.... Now she wants her children back."

There was absolutely nothing she could say.

"Her babies." The words were barely a whisper. He was still staring at the far wall.

Sandy felt her eyes filling with tears, but she blinked furiously, determined not to cry. If Anne had taken a knife, stabbed Burt in the stomach and then twisted it, she couldn't have hurt him more deeply than she was hurting him now.

"But she let you have custody."

He let go of her hand and slid himself slowly up the couch until he was sitting in the far corner. She didn't rush to move next to him, sensing he didn't want that. Not now.

"You don't understand. Something sacred happens when a woman gets pregnant and has a child. That child came out of her body. She has a feeling for it no man can possibly understand."

She hated seeing him in this much pain.

"Anne's mother called me almost two months ago and told me she would do this. I called up the lawyer her lawyer recommended. No matter what I do, Michael and Ryan lose."

When she didn't say anything, he continued, one of his hands supporting his forehead as if he were in physical pain.

"They're not considered adults until they're eighteen years old or out of high school. They can't choose which parent they'd like to live with until they're twelve. The law in this state gives the natural mother every possible break because a child should be with his mother.''

He took a deep breath, and she could almost feel the pain in his chest.

''If I fight to retain custody, I'm going to have to drag Anne through dirt. I'm not sure I care about her at all anymore. But it would kill me to do it to Michael. He still loves her. And she's still Ryan's mother, too, even if he isn't as close.''

''Burt, perhaps you could come to some agreement before—''

''You don't understand Anne. She gets crazy. I mean absolutely crazy. She's probably almost halfway into her pregnancy by now, and it's only going to get worse.''

''Did you eat any dinner?'' She grasped at something tangible. Something this enormous could be handled only a little at a time. Burt looked terrible. There was a tightness around his mouth and pain in his eyes. All she could think of was to help him, take care of him.

''I don't want anything. I'm sorry it happened this weekend.''

''I'm sorry it happened at all.'' She moved slightly closer. ''I'd still like to stay with you. If you want me here.''

''It won't be what you thought it was going to be.''

''I know that. Come on, Burt, let's get you to bed. I'll make something for you to eat— Don't say no. You can't be like this when the boys get home; you'll scare them to death.''

He closed his eyes tightly.

"That's what gets me the most. I've watched them both for such a long time. From the first moment Anne and I started having trouble, then Anne left, and then the divorce. Ryan hasn't had a normal day from the moment he was born.

"I thought they'd adjust a little better if everything didn't change, so I fought for the house and agreed to pay Anne her share. I made sure they had their same rooms, tried to do all the right things. I've watched them change from two frightened little kids into two terrific boys. And I thought most of it was behind us. I thought the most difficult thing was going to be having to tell them about the new baby."

She thought of all the things she could say, of telling him that with his love as a foundation, Michael and Ryan would weather this, too. But it all sounded so meaningless. If Anne took the children away, it would be a tragedy for everyone concerned.

Help me, she thought silently. *Help me help him.* And her mind flashed back to that spring day, and the look in her twin's eyes as she sat next to him for those last minutes.

No matter how bad it gets, it's still the greatest gift of all.

"Come on. Bed. You've been hit with a terrible shock and you need to rest. You can't do anything just now, so I want you to try and sleep."

She said the words briskly, hoping to bluff Burt into believing one of them was strong, and to her amazement he slowly rose to his feet. She held out her hand, took his and walked with him back to the bedroom.

HE SLEPT for most of the night. Sandy fixed them
sandwiches and mugs of soup, woke him briefly and
insisted he eat. After the thrown-together dinner, she
swept up as much of the glass as she could, then vac-
uumed the carpet and tried to put the den back in order.

What was left of the glass bookshelf was in ruins, so
she rummaged around the kitchen until she found
some heavy gloves and worked out the broken pieces
of glass that were still inside the shelf, then wrapped
them in a separate bag and carried them out to the
garbage.

Most of the pictures were still all right, frames intact. She wiped them off carefully, then set them on
the now upright coffee table.

The only picture damaged beyond repair was the
wedding portrait. The picture itself was still intact, but
the silver frame had been gouged, the glass shattered.
Knowing Burt would want it again someday, if only
for his children, Sandy threw away the loose glass and
set it inside one of the drawers in the heavy oak desk
in the den.

Then, thinking of Ryan, she went back to his bedroom and checked on Hambo. The hamster was up,
running furiously on his wheel. She checked to make
sure he had food and water, then closed Ryan's bedroom door and walked back down the hallway to the
den.

She wasn't sleepy, and certainly didn't want to disturb Burt. Television and music didn't appeal to her,
either. She felt restless, full of pent-up emotion she
didn't know what to do with.

Sandy thought briefly of going home, but she didn't want to leave Burt completely alone when he was this vulnerable. She walked into the kitchen, thinking she might simply get her weekend bag, prepare for bed and sleep in the guest room, when she thought of the pool.

It was a hot summer night, and a brief swim would relax her, help her sleep.

Swiftly changing into her brief black suit, she slipped on flip-flops and grabbed one of Burt's old toweling robes she found hanging on the back of the door. She didn't think he'd mind if she used it.

The backyard was dark, the only illumination coming from the single bulb above the back steps. Wadsworth trotted contentedly beside her. He seemed happy with her company.

She set the robe on one of the chaise lounges, slipped off her flip-flops, then walked over to the diving board. Stepping up on the rough surface, she moved to the middle of the board and looked up at the summer sky.

This high up in the hills, she could see stars twinkling faintly. She wondered if Michael was lying in his sleeping bag, looking up at those same stars. She had been to Idyllwild only once, the first summer after Jimmy died. She'd learned how to ride a motorcycle, gotten her license, bought her bike with some of the money he had left her and spent every single weekend running as far away as she could.

Sandy glanced back down at the water. It was dark, seemingly bottomless. The tiny slice of new moon silvered the water ever so slightly.

She took three steps forward, bounced up off the board, and entered the water cleanly. It was cool, and felt good against her skin. When she surfaced at the far end of the pool, she turned around and began to swim laps.

Sandy was still swimming when she became aware of someone in the water with her. She stopped, then treaded water until Burt surfaced next to her.

"You were right," he said. "I'm not doing anyone any good by going off the deep end."

"You needed to get it out of your system."

"You shouldn't be swimming alone."

"Nothing would have happened to me. I was being careful."

"Let's swim for a while."

It was a relief to be engaged in something physical, moving her body, pushing herself so the tension gave way and she began to feel better.

When she tired, Sandy swam to the shallow end, then walked up the steps and, grasping her hair, gently squeezed the water out of it. Burt was still swimming, back and forth, so she reached for the robe, wrapped it around her and lay down in the lounge chair.

Burt joined her after a while, clad in another toweling robe. He pulled a lounge chair close to hers and sat down.

"Look at the stars," she said softly. "I can see the Big Dipper."

"One summer," Burt said, "Michael and I brought out the sleeping bags and laid them in the backyard. We must have stayed out here for a couple of hours. He used to love to have me point out the different constellations."

"Do you still know where they all are?"

"Sure."

She sat with him as he pointed out the stars, and her heart ached. She could picture Burt and Michael lying on sleeping bags, exploring the summer skies. Burt was so infinitely patient with his children. She'd never known a man who enjoyed being a father more.

"Are you tired?" he asked her, after a while.

"No."

"I'm glad you chose to stay."

"So am I."

"I'm kind of hungry. What about you?"

"Soup's not very filling." She smiled. One step at a time.

"We could take a shower, then go to this all-night deli on Ventura."

"Only if we take my motorcycle."

"You're on."

BURT HAD RIDDEN MOTORCYCLES before, so they had no trouble making their way down the hill to Ventura Boulevard and finding the deli. Afterward, as they walked outside, the sky was just beginning to lighten.

Sandy was walking beside Burt, holding his hand, when she thought of the perfect way to start their day.

"Let's go to the beach and watch the sun rise."

"Now?"

"This second."

As they were getting on her motorcycle and she handed Burt her spare helmet, she said, "You'll have to hold on tight. I'll have to speed a little if we're going to make it."

"Just don't take any chances."

She loved riding to the ocean. From the valley the route was slightly different. West on Ventura, then south on Sepulveda. They eased onto 405 South, then hooked up to 10 West.

It was her favorite way of first seeing the ocean, coming out from under the overpass and suddenly being on Pacific Coast Highway going north, the ocean stretching away on their left side as far as you could see.

A brisk ocean breeze was blowing, and she was glad they had both worn heavy jackets for protection. They sped up past the colorful houses in Malibu, and when they reached the parking lot by Zuma Beach, she pulled the bike over and came to a stop.

After stowing their helmets away and putting the lock on the bike, they walked across the concrete, then onto white sand and all the way to the water.

The first faint rays of dawn were just beginning to come up over the hills, streaking the sky with pastel colors.

"It's always beautiful at this time," she said, taking his hand as they began to walk along the shoreline.

"I haven't been here in a while. George and Alice have been taking the boys to the beach this summer. I'm going to have to get in there and do my share."

"They know you're on a deadline."

"And Alice knows I like having time with you. I think you two are going to really like each other."

He explained their history as they walked, occasionally stopping to look at small shells or watch sea birds.

"I used to come here all the time with Jimmy when we were kids." They had started to head back up toward the motorcycle, but now Burt put a restraining hand on her arm and she stopped.

"Tell me about him."

And she smiled up into his face, realizing it was the perfect place. She never felt closer to her brother than when she walked along the shoreline.

They walked up from the waves and sat down on the firmly packed sand close to the water. Sandy leaned her head against Burt's shoulder and tucked her hand through his arm.

"He was just the person I was always closest to. My mom used to say we started playing in the womb and never stopped."

"Do you have any other brothers and sisters?"

"One older brother, Bo. I think he felt left out a lot of the time because Jimmy and I were so close."

"Fraternal twins."

"We just did everything together. Got into trouble, played, stuck up for each other. He was like the other side of me, my other half. He was so great, Burt. Even when Jimmy got to be that age where brothers hate having sisters, he was never that way to me. We just loved being together."

She felt his hand cover hers, squeezing her fingers, urging her to continue.

"When I was fifteen, my mother and I were shopping when this woman came up and asked if I'd be interested in doing some print modeling. I couldn't have cared less one way or another, and my mom was never one to push, but Jimmy convinced me it would be this great adventure, so I decided to do it. We were always daring each other to do things, not anything harmful, but we'd always call each other on being scared, stuff like that.''

"I know what you mean. My brother, Chris, and I used to do the same thing."

"So I started. Burt, I was almost five-eight by the time I was a freshman in high school. I always felt like a giraffe next to all these short boys." She smiled. "I told Jimmy I wanted to be one of those little girls who could sit on a boy's lap and not crush him to death."

"You don't crush me."

"I really loved it, that first night when you picked me up and carried me into your bedroom. No one had ever done that to me before."

"I'll keep that in mind. So, you started modeling."

"Yeah, and it gave me this kind of superficial confidence. You know, I knew how to use makeup and wear certain types of clothing. I began to feel like I looked good. Jimmy used to tease me all the time, but I knew he was proud of me. Mom and Dad and Bo were, too. We didn't have a ton of money when I was growing up, so I felt really proud to be contributing.

"When I graduated from high school, I didn't see any sense in going to college when I was making good money and could make more. So I kept at it. Jimmy wanted to go to USC, and I wanted to help him."

"What did he want to be?"

"A doctor. When we were kids, he was always finding banged-up baby birds and frogs and things. He was just fascinated with life. He would have made a great doctor, not one of those cold, intimidating types. Jimmy could talk to anyone.

"So I modeled and he went to college. Bo was married by then, and none of us was living at home. And as I kept modeling—'' her hand tightened on his arm ''—I fell in with this crowd. Nobody forced me to do anything, but I was always really curious, and deep inside I still felt like I was this enormous, gawky girl that no one would ever ask to dance. Do you know what I mean?''

"I do. Never measuring up."

"Exactly. So I fell in with this crowd, with this guy. I fell in love with him and moved in with him. My mother thought I was living in this apartment with two other girls, but I was living with Gary.

"It was just such a messed-up time in my life. I thought the coolest people were up for anything at any time. I was having trouble keeping my weight down, and he—Gary—gave me some pills. I was just so strung out for almost a year and a half of my life. I look back on it, Burt, and I don't even know why. I was pretending to everyone that I knew exactly what I was doing but I didn't have any idea what I wanted to do with my life. I admired my brothers. Bo was raising a family, Jimmy was working toward helping people. And I was just a mess.

"I don't think my mom and dad ever knew, or if they did, they didn't let on. But I think they would have said something about it. Bo suspected, but he was busy with his own life. Jimmy knew right away. He blamed himself. He said I never would have been under so much pressure if I hadn't agreed to help him through school.

"I didn't want to disappoint him, so I cleaned up my act. A little. But it wasn't for me. Everything I did was for other people, you know? So I kept modeling and bringing in all this money, taking more and more jobs. I was always a really healthy kid, had great stamina. I look back and I don't even know how I got through that time, I was so messed up. I didn't take care of myself, didn't sleep. But I managed to show up at work.

"I'd been modeling for about two years when my mom called me and told me I had to come home. Jimmy was sick. I stopped everything and went home. He had cancer. I don't know how or why— I've gone over it a million times in my head. I watched him die. I didn't do much of anything else, just spent time with Jimmy. We went to so many doctors, but it was bone cancer and it had spread too far and there was nothing they could do. Not at that time."

She cleared her throat. "And I used to think, why wasn't it me? I was doing nothing but screwing up my life royally, and here it was Jimmy dying. I didn't understand that.

"But it straightened me out. It was like, I watched him die and I learned how to live. You know those articles about people beating death? Everything's true. You look at things a whole new way."

She stopped talking, her throat tight, then swallowed and continued.

"One of the last days I spent with Jimmy, we were laughing, but then he got serious and he made me promise not to waste an hour of my life. Not a day. And to always take risks to get to my goals. Burt, he was *dying*, and he used to look at me and smile and say these crazy things like, 'I don't understand what people mean by spare time. There's no such thing as spare time. There's just time, and life, and that's the greatest gift there is.' He just turned my head around and there was no going back.

"All that stuff you hear about life being too short—I never understood until he died. The very last day, he was sitting outside in the backyard. Jimmy wanted to die at home, so we brought him home from the hospital before he couldn't leave. My dad had to carry him outside. He was in a lot of pain.

"And I was sitting next to him, and he told me the biggest mistake he'd made was thinking he'd live until he was really old. And he told me not to make the same mistake, because life doesn't offer you any guarantees. He told me to take big risks, push ahead when I was scared, and be of use to others.

"We sat out in the backyard and I put my arm around him like I used to do when we were little, and he died."

He handed her a handkerchief and she blew her nose. They sat watching the ocean for several minutes, then Sandy said quietly, "The thing I learned that day is that you can die at any minute. And the second you face up to that, you have a lot less trouble figuring out what you want to do with your life. You're still scared to do it, but deep inside, you know."

"What did you decide?"

"I didn't want to be a model, and I didn't want to hang out with Gary's crowd. I didn't want that lifestyle. I quit everything when I found out how sick Jimmy was, but after he died, I thought about what he'd said. I knew I liked people and I loved animals, especially dogs. So I began checking out ways I could work with dogs and took a training program at the place where I work, and now I help people with their dogs. It's not saving the world, but I love doing it."

She felt Burt's arm around her, comforting and strong, as he hugged her close against him.

"And once a month, I take a few dogs over to the children's ward at Hollywood Presbyterian. There's an orphanage in Santa Monica I visit, and a senior citizens' home in Burbank. I take Panda, my dog, and Elaine's dog, Lola, and two others whose owners let me borrow them for the day."

"You never told me this."

"I wanted to tell you all at once. It doesn't make sense any other way. I'm not this naturally nice person, Burt. I was this screwed-up, crazy kid, and I've come to believe that Jimmy was born with me to teach me how to live. Not just for me; I don't mean it selfishly. But it's just that his death had such an impact on my life."

"And that's why you're the person you are. But give yourself some credit, Sandy. Another person might have gone through the same thing and not learned anything."

"I couldn't not learn. I loved him so much and it hurt all the time, seeing him dying. And I miss him. Every single day."

They were quiet for some time, then Burt spoke. "Sandy?"

She looked up at him.

"Thanks for sharing Jimmy with me."

"He would have liked you." She leaned her cheek against his shoulder.

Chapter Twelve

"Drink your champagne."

Sandy turned her attention back to Burt. She'd been glancing around the tiny interior of the Seventh Street Bistro. It was a darling restaurant, done in shades of eggshell gray and blue, very French. And obviously very expensive.

"This is our first real official date, if you don't count the deli."

He smiled at her, champagne flute in hand. "Let's make a toast."

She picked up her own. "I like that idea."

"To us. To this exact moment in time, and to Wadsworth, man's best matchmaker."

Sandy raised the flute of champagne to her lips, her eyes never leaving his. She loved champagne, the way the bubbles filled your mouth, the clean taste. It made everything so special.

Something caught her eye. She looked at the delicate glass. There, at the bottom in the midst of all the tiny bubbles— "Burt?" Her voice quavered.

He was grinning now. "Fish it out."

"Oh, Burt!"

He laughed softly as she drank more of her champagne, then maneuvered the ring carefully out of the delicate glass. Sandy dried it on her napkin, then held the ring between her fingers and stared at the diamond.

"Burt, it's beautiful."

"Let me put it on."

He slid it onto her finger. She couldn't stop looking at him, her heart in her eyes. He kept her hand in his as he spoke.

"Sandy, I love you like I've loved no other woman in my life. I know I want to spend the rest of my life with you." His voice was low, intense. "Will you marry me?"

She couldn't speak through sudden tears, could only nod her head. Her decision came straight from the heart. She had no hesitation.

His face was alight with happiness. Then he squeezed her hand and said softly, "Will you do something else for me?"

She nodded.

"After this weekend, will you go home and really think about your answer for a couple of days?"

"I don't have to. I know it's the right one."

"Would you do it for me?"

"If you want me to."

"I do." His gaze was steady as he looked at her. "You're walking into one hell of a situation. I have two children who may end up needing a tremendous amount of time and love from me, and right now I have to be there for them."

"Burt, I know that. It's one of the reasons I love you."

"I just want you to be sure. I've thought about this a lot, and in some ways you deserve better. A guy you could start out fresh with, someone without all the complications I'll be bringing to a marriage."

"But I've already fallen in love with the best man in the entire world." She squeezed his hand. "I know Michael and Ryan probably won't like it at first. Being your friend is totally different from having them accept me as your wife. I'll never expect them to look at me as their mother, but I'll try to be their friend. I know it'll be a difficult adjustment. But it's just that I happen to think you're the most wonderful man, and that makes up for anything life might throw our way."

"But you'll still think about it. Promise me that."

"I will. But don't bet on me changing my mind. I love you, Burt. The feelings I have for you aren't going to go away."

"But think about it."

"I will. I promise."

He poured them more champagne as they waited for their dinner to arrive. Sandy kicked off her heels beneath the table and slid one silk-clad foot against Burt's ankle.

He caught her eye and smiled.

"What are you up to?"

"I thought I might liven things up before dinner. A kind of appetizer, something to stimulate the senses."

He was still smiling as she slid her leg slowly up his muscled calf.

"You're going to drive me crazy."

"You catch on quickly." She reached for her champagne glass, as if they were having the most ordinary conversation in the world, then glanced around the table to make sure no one was within listening range. "I thought you might like to know what Elaine brought me back from London."

"Something along the lines of that bathing suit, I hope."

"Better." She described the silk teddy to him in loving detail, watching his eyes darken and the smile slowly leave his face to be replaced with an expression of pure desire.

He caught her foot with his hand as it inched higher.

"Are you wearing it right now?"

She nodded.

Their waiter came to the table at that exact moment and set their first course in front of them.

When he left, Burt gave her foot a gentle squeeze before he released it.

"Lady, you're going to pay."

She was laughing as she picked up her fork.

THEY SPENT THE REST of the weekend in bed.

"There is nothing as sexy," Sandy said late Sunday afternoon, "as being naked in bed with the man you love, wearing nothing but an engagement ring."

"I think that teddy comes in a close second." Burt was lying next to her in bed, his hand warm on her back.

"Elaine thought you'd like it. She asked me to tell you it was a present for you, too."

"Make sure you thank her for me."

"I will." She laughed. "I never told you this. That Saturday when I brought a swimsuit over? She switched suits on me. I never would have worn that black suit so soon."

"I'm going to have to pay Elaine a visit and thank her in person."

"Oh, she liked you from the start. Especially when I told her you looked like Tom Berenger."

"Get out of here."

"It's true. Elaine was determined to play matchmaker." She started to laugh.

"What's so funny? It worked."

Still laughing, she told him about Fred and Elaine and the roundabout love affair that had been going on since Fred had moved into the guest house.

"I'm almost afraid of what I'll find when I get back. I hope the house is still standing."

He laughed, then drew her tightly against him.

SHE LEFT before Michael and Ryan returned, promising Burt she would think about his proposal for two days. When she returned home, the house was strangely quiet. Sandy dumped her bag on the floor by her bed, petted Panda and told her how much she'd missed her, then changed into a white cotton nightgown and crawled into her bed, exhausted.

Before she had left, she'd told Burt to call her any time during the two days she was going to spend apart from him. She was worried about him, knowing that the thought of Anne taking Michael and Ryan away was never far from his mind.

But now, in the quiet and comfort of her own bedroom, she closed her eyes and slept.

"SANDY! SANDY, ARE YOU AWAKE?"

She opened one eye in time to see Elaine stagger into her bedroom, then close the door and lean against it.

Early morning light was streaming in the bedroom windows.

"Elaine, are you all right?" She sat up in bed, suddenly awake.

Her friend laughed, then rolled her eyes. She looked incredibly vibrant, her long hair loose and fluffed around her face, her eyes bright. There was a good amount of color in her cheeks, and her lips looked as if she had been thoroughly kissed.

"Sandy, I can't even *begin* to tell you what happened this weekend."

"Fred?" she said hopefully.

Elaine nodded, then pushed herself forward and began to walk toward the bed. Sandy scooted to one side as Elaine fell, face forward, onto her coverlet.

"And Fred, and Fred, and Fred," she muttered, sounding happily exhausted. "I never would have suspected that underneath that funny, happy-go-lucky exterior lies the soul of a sex maniac."

Sandy started to laugh.

"He's a Scorpio," Elaine muttered. "With Scorpio rising—if you know what I mean."

Sandy buried her face in a pillow to stifle her laughter.

"And now I have to go to Germany and check out eye pencils."

"Look at it this way—you have something to look forward to when you return."

"It was amazing. We went to this Italian restaurant after he performed, then we both drank all this wine, and when we got home, well . . . he performed again."

"Who made the first move?"

"I think he did. I don't know. From Friday night to Monday morning is all one big blur."

"There's a happy man resting in the guest house."

"Mmm. I've got to throw myself into a cold shower and get dressed. My plane leaves at eleven. Oh, God—"

"Get going. You can do it."

"I'm going to sleep on the entire flight."

"I'm happy for you, Elaine."

"How was your weekend with the big B?"

"I'll tell you when you get back. Get moving, you're going to be late."

MUCH LATER IN THE MORNING Sandy woke to hear a soft scratching at the door.

"Come in, Panda."

Panda looked up from the rug by her bed and whined.

"Sandy." A muffled voice came from behind the door.

"Fred?" She sat up in bed, then watched as Fred came crawling around the door.

"It worked," he said, then sprawled on her carpet, rolling over onto his back, his eyes closed.

She bit her lip against the laughter bubbling inside.

"I would have never suspected that inside my Elaine, my college pal, my bosom buddy, beats the heart of a...tigress. It was wonderful."

"What happened?"

"We went to this Italian restaurant after my show, then afterward...Elaine put on quite a show of her own."

"Which one of you made the first move?"

"She did. I think. I don't know. From Friday night to Monday morning is all—"

"One big blur."

"One big wonderful blur." He opened one bleary eye and glanced at her. "How was your weekend?"

"The best. I'm getting married."

He opened his other eye and stared at her. "I would run over and hug you and then jump up and down for joy, but I think it would kill me." He took a deep breath. "I'm really happy for you, Sandy."

"Just think, you and Elaine will eventually have this house all to yourselves."

He sighed. "It may just kill me. But what a way to go!"

LYING IN BED that evening, Burt felt a peculiar kind of peace.

Michael and Ryan were in bed. They had talked about their trip all evening, and it had been very clear they'd both had a terrific time. Michael told him all about the different stars he'd seen, and even Ryan forgot Hambo long enough to tell him he'd seen a rabbit.

Now, alone in bed, he thought of Anne. And Sandy. And Jimmy.

He could take this new twist in his life and let it rule him, make him fearful about the next day, the next week or month. Or he could choose to live completely in the present and let both his sons know how much he loved them.

The answer was perfectly clear.

His head came up when he heard the soft knock at the door.

"Dad?" It was Michael.

"Come in."

He opened the door, then stepped inside, looking cautiously toward the bed.

"Sandy's not here tonight, Michael."

"Can I sit with you?"

Michael had always asked, even as a child. Almost as if he were never really sure he would be welcome. Ryan merely tumbled ahead.

"Sure."

He moved over as Michael climbed up on the bed, then lay down against the pillow.

He decided to let his son speak first.

"Dad, is something wrong?"

Michael had always had emotional radar. And here he'd thought he'd kept his feelings under control.

He couldn't lie to him.

"How would you like to live with your mother?"

"Would you come, too?"

"No."

"I'd live with that guy?"

"I think so."

Michael was silent for a minute, taking this in.

"How do you feel about it?" Burt asked.

"Kind of scared. Where would Ryan go?"

"He'd go with you."

"Would you come visit?"

"All the time."

He sighed, and Burt wished with all his heart that he'd never had to put these questions to his child.

"Does she want me back?"

The question tore at his heart. He knew what the divorce had done to his son, making him feel as if he were an emotional Ping-Pong ball, being bounced from one parent to another. He and Ryan visited Anne, and Burt had found out after several of those visits that she talked with Michael all the time about coming to live with her. Then she wouldn't bring up the subject for the next few visits.

No wonder he was confused.

"I think so. But I need to know what you want, Michael. I know it's really hard for you, but I need you to tell me the truth."

There were tears standing out in his eyes.

"I want . . . I want to stay here with you."

"Okay."

"Then I can?"

"I hope so. I'm going to see what I can do. There are some laws that may make it impossible, but I'll fight as hard as I can to see that you live where you want to. And I want you to know, Michael, that I hate this as much as you do, and I get scared, too."

"You do?"

"Yeah. I want you and Ryan and me to stay to-gether, and I'm not sure it's going to be possible. But I'm going to talk to your mother and tell her what you said and try to work something out. And if you feel like something's wrong with me, it's not anything you've done. I've just got a lot on my mind. And whatever you want to ask me, ask."

Michael had slowly inched over on the bed, and now Burt put his arm around his son and gently pulled him closer.

"Sometimes she scares me," Michael said.

"I know. She scares me, too."

DURING THE TWO DAYS she was apart from Burt, Sandy thought of him constantly. Monday she slept in and did laundry, then several errands. Tuesday she visited a home for abused children. The woman who ran the orphanage in Santa Monica had given her information about this particular institution, and Sandy had decided to add it to her list.

She borrowed Elaine's other car, a Honda station wagon, loaded the dogs in and drove down to Long Beach.

Inside, she watched as her animal friends worked their particular brand of magic.

"What's her name?" asked one little boy.

"Panda. Sometimes I call her Panda Bear."

"Come here, Panda Bear!"

And Panda, the gentlest dog Sandy had ever owned, trotted over to the little boy and swiped at his face with her tongue. He pulled at her airplane ears, and she merely wagged her plumed tail.

Lola, the Lhasa apso, loved children and they adored her. Something about the fluffy white dog made everyone want to pet her. She was the cutest of the four. Snoopy, a six-year-old beagle, charmed his way into everyone's heart. And Sam, a short, stubby, fluffy mutt, was an absolute rock.

Sandy had worked out a little skit with the four dogs, in which they all went to school and had to perform various tricks. Lola danced. Panda jumped through a hoop. Snoopy delivered a letter to one of the children in the audience and Sam begged for treats, a basket in his mouth.

Afterward, the dogs all on leashes, one of the nuns walked her outside.

"I can't tell you how much the children enjoyed that skit. I hope you'll come back again."

"Just say the word." Sandy stopped beside the Honda's hatchback. She'd parked the car in the shade so it wouldn't be too uncomfortable for the dogs. Now she opened the back of the car and all four began to clamber in. She lifted Sam. He was getting old and was too fat to jump.

"Did you see the little girl in the pink dress?"

"Yes. She was darling. She really liked Snoopy."

"We've been trying to get her to talk for weeks. When Snoopy gave her that letter, she patted him and I heard her say 'dog.'"

"I'll tell you, these guys are miracle workers. 'Angels in fur,' my brother used to say."

"Could I tell her you'll be back? I think it would help."

"I'll come back next Tuesday."

"Sandy, you're sure? I couldn't let them get their hopes up and have you not come."

"You can count on me."

Driving home, the air conditioner on full blast, she thought of Burt. She'd decided to call him Wednesday morning and ask him out to dinner. During the two days he had asked her to think about his proposal, she had weighed everything in her mind, gone over everything that could possibly go wrong, thought about all the problems they would have to face.

But it always came back to Burt. She could not separate the man she loved from the father who cared so intensely, and she would never want to try. There would be problems. Michael would test both of them, push them to their limits in order to make sure his father's remarriage wouldn't mean his own abandonment. But as long as she understood, and as long as she had Burt by her side, she could face anything.

ELAINE HAD SUGGESTED REX, an Italian restaurant on Olive between Sixth and Seventh streets. A former haberdashery from the twenties, the place had an Art Deco atmosphere.

Fred dropped Sandy off in front, and she smiled at the doorman as she walked in. She wore a simple gray silk dress, and had French-braided her hair down her back.

Burt was already at the table she had reserved and he looked up as she slid into the seat across from him.

"Hi." He seemed nervous.

"Hi. How was the camping trip?"

They talked easily through before-dinner drinks. But Burt was on edge. Sandy didn't question her instincts. He'd glanced at her hand when she first picked up her drink, and seemed relieved that she was still wearing the ring he had given her.

He's scared. He thinks everything is going to frighten me away.

She decided to tell him her decision before they ordered. It would be too cruel to make him eat an entire meal wondering. Especially since he didn't seem to have a whole lot of faith in the outcome.

"Burt," she began softly. "I want you to know that what we have has been the most wonderful thing that's ever happened to me—"

"—but now it's time to say goodbye," he finished for her, his eyes dark.

She couldn't believe what she was hearing. "Wait a minute. That's not what I was going to say. Is that what you think I want to tell you?"

He seemed genuinely confused. "But I thought you brought me here because... Someone once told me the best way to break off a relationship was to do it in an elegant restaurant. That way the other person wouldn't dare make a scene. So when you called, I assumed—"

"Burt, I picked out this restaurant because I know you've been under a lot of pressure and I thought it would be nice for you to have a night away from everything. I didn't have any ulterior motive in mind!"

They were both silent for a minute. Their waiter approached their table.

"Would you like to order now?"

Neither of them had even looked at the menu.

"Give us just a few more minutes," Burt said.

"Of course."

"You should know me better than that," Sandy continued once their waiter was out of earshot. "I wouldn't care where we were; I'd cause a scene. And I have a feeling you would, too. Burt, why can't you believe I want to marry you?"

His eyes never left hers. "I've been doing a lot of thinking, Sandy. Looking back, I might have asked you to take that time to think because I needed it, too. I thought about what you would have to face, coming into this marriage. I can't see the problems with Anne ever ending, at least until both Michael and Ryan reach the age of consent. I don't know how they're going to take our marriage."

"I've thought about all of that, and I know I can deal with whatever happens, as long as you're with me. Burt, I *love* you. Love isn't just stepping back and offering someone a perfect life. Love is accepting someone just the way they are and working through life together, helping each other. I've never felt what I feel for you for any other man, and I want that feeling to deepen. I want to live with you, share my life with you—"

"Sandy, your whole life is spread out in front of you—"

"What is this? Are you going to start up that business of being ten years older than I am? Burt, you were married before. I'd have been surprised if you hadn't, at thirty-six. You have children. You know how I feel about them. I think the only problem I'm going to have is feeling so helpless while all this goes on with Anne. I'm going to have to depend on you to tell me how much I should get involved and when I should step back."

"But you shouldn't even have to fight these battles."

"Why does that bother you? Burt, love isn't worth anything if it can't get through rough times. I was a mess, a real mess, and Jimmy never stopped loving me. He never made it a conditional thing. 'Now while things are fine and you're behaving all right I think I'll choose to love you.' I was a mess, Burt, a selfish, self-absorbed idiot, and he stuck with me. And what do you think, that when he was dying I didn't have days when I wanted to walk out the door and keep going? It killed me to see him in so much pain. There were days when I used to want to scream. But I loved him,

Burt. I loved him so much I couldn't do that. Love makes all the difference. I think it's the only thing there is, in the end."

He didn't answer.

"I bet there are times when Michael and Ryan are real pains, but that doesn't mean you stop loving them. And I know you must have loved Anne; you tried so hard to make your marriage work. We can do it, Burt, if we both want it badly enough."

He swallowed, and his throat worked.

If we both want it badly enough.

Realization struck. "Are you scared?"

The tense expression on his face was her answer, and suddenly she knew that a part of him had hoped her answer would be no.

"Oh, Burt, I don't know what marriage is. The only thing I know is that I love you. I'm not Anne. It's not going to be like that. I'm scared, too. I knew from the beginning that we met at the wrong time."

"But life isn't perfect."

She could feel tears stinging her eyes. "Yeah. And there's only this moment, right now, you and me. No guarantees. Burt, I'm jumping in with both feet, and maybe I'm a lot more ignorant than you are about what we're getting into, but I have to know you're jumping with me."

"Sandy..." His voice was tight. Filled with pain.

"Please say something, Burt."

When he didn't answer, she swallowed, then spoke slowly. Painfully.

"You told me once," she said, twisting the ring carefully off her finger, "that you wanted me to think about my answer. I did. I thought about us the entire two days. And I thought about Michael and Ryan.''

She took a deep breath. "I want to marry you, Burt, but now I want you to take some time and think about whether *you* want this.'' She set the ring down between them.

He was silent, his eyes bright, his jaw tense.

"Don't answer me now. Take a week. Take a month. I know the pressure you're under, Burt, and I'm not playing a game with you. I love you, I'm not going anywhere. But I have to know you feel sure about this. As sure as you can ever feel about something like this.''

"Would you care to order now?'' The waiter had approached their table unobtrusively.

"No. I'm sorry. I don't have much of an appetite. I'm sorry, Burt.'' She set her napkin down on the table, stood up and walked away.

Her legs were shaking, her eyes burning. Just walking away from that table had been one of the hardest things she had ever done.

Once outside, when the valet came up and asked her which car was hers, she realized she had no way home.

She'd counted on being with Burt.

Turning, she asked the doorman quietly, "Could you call me a cab?''

He nodded.

BURT WATCHED HER as she walked away, the long line of her bare back, the proud angle of her head.

He knew he was afraid. He knew he didn't want Sandy to be exposed to the utter mess he had made of his life. His and his children's.

And he hadn't realized how guilty he still was until he hadn't been able to answer her.

She reminded him, in the craziest of ways, of Michael. Burt couldn't give either of them anything but honesty.

He sat looking down at the table, his mind racing. Remembering her face. Remembering their weekend. Strangely, what seemed clearest was their morning at the beach, sitting and talking.

Words she had said while leaning against his shoulder flitted through his memory.

He made me promise not to waste an hour of my life. Not a day. And to always take risks to get to my goals.

He thought of Sandy, of the joy he had felt when she had found the ring in the bottom of her champagne glass. And he picked up the ring, still warm from her hand. The diamond flashed fire in the subdued light.

He could almost hear her voice inside his head.

The thing I learned that day is that you can die at any minute. And the second you face up to that, you have a lot less trouble figuring out what you want to do with your life. You're still scared to do it, but deep inside, you know.

He was standing up, but he wasn't sure quite how he had gotten to his feet. Then he was walking, following the same path she had taken, his eyes searching ahead for the brightness of her hair.

When he got outside, he saw her. She was just stepping inside the back of a cab, and he was struck by the vulnerable line of her back.

"Sandy!"

She turned, her eyes filled with tears, the cab door still open.

He nodded his head, unsure of his voice, then started to run toward her.

The minute she was in his arms, the world fell back into place.

"Baby, I'm so sorry. I just—I *am* scared. I want this to be good for you. I want it to work. I love you, it's just sometimes I can't seem to find the words—"

Then he was kissing her, and she knew everything was right again. They loved each other; they would be together. It was all that was important.

A car horn honked, then the cab driver's voice cut into her consciousness.

"Lady, my meter's running."

She was smiling through her tears. "So's mine."

"Do you want this cab or not?"

"Yes." She gave the driver her address as Burt shut the door.

"My place is closer."

"Mmm-hmm." He was kissing her neck.

"We can come back for your car."

"Mmm."

"I wasn't that hungry, anyway."

"Forgive me."

"There's nothing to forgive. I love you." She leaned close, her lips against his ear. "I love you, I love you, I *love* you. That's all there is."

SEVERAL HOURS LATER she lay in her bed and watched Burt dress.

"I'll call you in the morning," he said. "We can start making plans right away. Do you want a big wedding?"

"Just you and me would be fine."

He smiled down at her as he knotted his tie. "And maybe a small reception later. It would help it seem real to Michael and Ryan."

"That sounds good."

He sat down on the edge of the bed. "Do you want to have children?"

She knew the importance of what he was asking her. "We have two children."

"You know what I mean."

"I want to have yours. Not right away. Would you mind?" Suddenly, she felt shy with him.

He pulled the covers back and spread his fingers out against her flat stomach. Her muscles contracted with pleasure at his touch.

"I think I could handle diapers and midnight feedings again. If you wanted to."

"We'll see." She looped her arms around his neck. "I love you."

He kissed her. Slowly. Deeply. When his lips left hers, they brushed against her ear. "I love you, too."

He was almost to the door when she asked him. "What made you change your mind?"

He hesitated. "I was sitting at that table, and it was the strangest thing. I kept thinking about you, and then I thought about our talk on the beach. About Jimmy. And what he said about not wasting even an hour. Taking risks. And then I found myself standing and walking after you. It was like I couldn't not do it, do you know what I mean?"

"I do."

"I wish I could stay with you."

"Me, too. I think I hear the cab." She got out of bed, walked over to him and cupped his face in her hands. "One last kiss."

Afterward he swatted her bare bottom lightly. "Get back in that bed. We have a lot to get done this next week, and you'll need all your strength."

"I can't imagine why."

She listened as his footsteps faded down the hallway, then waited until she heard the sound of the car driving away. Her bedroom was dark now, the only illumination coming from the moonlight spilling through the windows.

A breeze ruffled the curtains, and she smiled.

And then I found myself standing and walking after you. It was like I couldn't not do it.

"I owe you one, Jimmy," she said softly. She could visualize his smile so clearly, feel the warmth of his love.

"If it's a boy, we'll name him after you." She turned over on her stomach and closed her eyes, content and ready to sleep.

"Or maybe," she said, just before she dropped off, "I'll really surprise Burt and have twins."

Epilogue

Five years later

"Sandy, what do you think of this one?" Michael held out a light blue cable-knit sweater.

"I think it would look great with those pants. Jonathan, baby, hold still. I just have to tack this one little piece." The four-year-old boy looked at her solemnly as she fastened his cowboy chaps to his jeans with a needle and thread. "I didn't think they'd keep falling off."

"Are you going to see Pat-ty at this par-ty?" Ryan teased Michael as he peeked around the doorway leading into the den.

"Shut up, butthead," Michael snapped.

Ryan started to laugh, and was joined in his hilarity by Chris Crowley, who was going to be spending the night.

Michael looked at Sandy. "He's just such a jerk."

She merely smiled.

"Mom," Ryan said as he burst into the den again, "Jamie's making a mess with her apple sauce. Wadsworth and Panda are licking it off the floor."

"Ryan, watch her just a second until I finish this."

"I've got her." Burt walked calmly into the den, his apple-sauce-spattered daughter in his arms. He sat down on the couch and began wiping the baby's face with a damp washcloth. "Ryan, what is it exactly that you and Chris have planned for this evening?"

Both boys started to laugh.

"Uncle Burt," Jonathan said quietly. "Sandy said I look like a cowboy. Do you think I look like a cowboy?"

"Let me see." Burt had grown accustomed to being called uncle. Anne and Carter's son, Jonathan was not truly his nephew, but Burt loved the boy. He inspected Jonathan's Halloween costume carefully. "Those chaps look mighty fine to me. And I like that hat. Yep, I think you'll make a fine cowboy."

Sandy glanced up at her husband. "We should get going before it gets too late."

"Okay. Now, who's going where?"

"I'm going to that party with Jeff," Michael said. "His older brother is driving."

"Whoa, wait. Do I know this guy?"

"Dad, you met him at the track meet that day. Steve Rush. You remember."

"When will he be here?"

"Any second."

"Bring him in the house. I'd like to meet him again."

Sandy watched the dismay in Michael's face at being treated like a baby. She'd met Steve at the same track meet.

"Michael, is he a safe driver?"

"Yeah, Sandy. He's a junior!"

"A stunning recommendation," Burt said under his breath, for her ears alone. Sandy smiled.

"But you think he's a good driver."

"Yeah."

"I remember him, Burt. You don't have to have him come in."

Michael flashed her a quick look of gratitude, then raced to his room, sweater in hand.

"Okay now, Ryan, what is it you and Chris are going to do?" Burt glanced at his son, who was looking at his friend with a guarded expression on his face. "Nothing destructive, I hope."

"No, Dad."

"George was mad as hell about that windshield, Ryan."

"No, Dad, nothing like that. We're just going to go out on our bikes for a little bit."

Burt gave him a look that made it quite clear he wasn't fooled, then said quietly, "Be careful."

"We will. Mom, if we get back by eight, can we watch movies with you and Dad?"

"Sure. We're only going to take Jonathan up and down the block."

"For candy," Jonathan reminded her.

Once Ryan and Chris slammed out the front door, the house was a little quieter.

"Just let me get a sweater on, Burt, and we're ready to go."

"What is Jamie going to be?" Jonathan piped up.

"A pumpkin," Burt said. "She's my little pumpkin."

Sandy walked Jonathan up to each house on the block and watched as he opened his bag and collected his Halloween candy. Burt stayed on the sidewalk, the dogs at his side and Jamie in his arms. Jonathan was coming along. Anne's marriage hadn't lasted long after his birth, and she had developed a habit of dropping him off with them for long periods of time. It was strange, because Jonathan looked like Anne, so he and Michael were taken for brothers more often than he and Ryan were.

She walked Jonathan up to another house, thankful that she and Alice had gotten together with some of the mothers on the block so all the children could trick-or-treat safely. And she smiled as Mrs. Waters oohed and aahed over Jonathan's costume.

Later, back at the house, Sandy lay back on the couch in the den. Jonathan had eaten some of his candy, and now, dressed in his pajamas, was watching *Star Wars*. Burt was in the bathroom, giving Jamie her bath.

She closed her eyes, exhausted. The past five years had raced along at breakneck speed. Burt had forestalled Anne's first custody attempt, but after Jonathan's birth she had started up again and both boys had ended up living with her for a couple of months. Burt had been devastated, but Sandy had trusted her instincts and encouraged him to hang in and wait. Her hunch had been proven right. When Anne's marriage had fallen apart, she had turned up with both boys and given them back to Burt. Jonathan had first come to visit when he was eight months old. When he turned two, the visits became four- and six-month stays.

Neither of them was really sure what Anne planned on doing with him.

But as long as he could stand the confusion in the Thomson house, he was welcome. Burt was wonderful with Jonathan, and Sandy's admiration for her husband had grown as she had watched him encourage the little boy to come out of his shell.

Burt had continued to write his John Savage series, but wrote about his father every other day until he'd finished an eight-hundred-page manuscript. He decided not to publish it, but had not destroyed it in case any of his three children might want to read it someday.

He and Alice had taken an evening class in writing screenplays. It had been Alice's idea, but the instructor had fired Burt up and he had worked on turning selected incidents in his manuscript into a screenplay. With the help of the instructor, a man who wrote both feature films and television movies of the week, Burt's screenplay had been optioned. He was working on another.

But perhaps the biggest surprise that had rocked the block over the past five years was Cecilia Forrest's arrest. A private investigator had tracked her down and proven she had murdered all three of her former husbands. Though Sandy had felt horrible for the men involved, she had been in a hysterical laughing fit when Burt burst in the door that day. Cici's house had been surrounded by squad cars.

"What the hell is going on out there?" he'd demanded.

In between fits and starts of laughter, she had told him about Cici.

"Sandy, you're talking about *murder*! What's so funny?"

"Because she poisoned them with her mu—her muff—her muffins."

Even Burt hadn't been able to keep a straight face after that. She had seen the funny look on his face over dinner, and within a short time he had sold a script with a similar idea to *Murder, She Wrote*.

And she had had her hands full, whether training dogs, listening to one of Burt's ideas and offering suggestions, visiting orphanages and nursing homes, looking out for the children, or feeding the dogs and Ryan's rapidly growing collection of hamsters. It was a never-ending circus, and she thrived on it.

She smiled when she felt Burt sit down on the couch beside her. He leaned over and kissed her.

"Jamie's ready for her good-night kiss."

She opened her eyes. Her daughter, fresh and apple-sauce-free in her sleeper, smiled.

"I'll take her in," Sandy offered, then groaned.

"Lie still. I have a plan."

Sandy kissed her daughter good-night, then Burt left. He came back within five minutes and knelt down, putting his lips close to her ear.

"I'm going to carry you back to bed so you can take a nap."

"Wonderful," she murmured.

"Then," he continued as he carried her down the hall, "I'll get Jonathan to sleep. Chris called and said he and Ryan are staying over at his house—I'm sure I'll find out why in the morning. In the meantime you'll have slept for an hour, and when I wake you up we'll have almost two more hours before Michael gets home."

"Burt, I'm so sorry. It's just that I was up at seven making that costume. I'll feel better once I sleep."

He undressed her, then tucked her into their king-size bed.

"Burt?"

"What is it, baby?"

"John Savage has nothing on you. He couldn't have planned a revolution more carefully."

He laughed.

An hour later Sandy woke up to find Burt easing the door open, balancing a tray in his hands.

He set it down on the bedside table, and she saw it held fluted glasses and a bottle of chilled champagne.

"I can't believe it!" She sat up in bed, clad only in her underwear and a T-shirt.

"Believe it." Burt started to open the bottle.

"Wait." Sandy ran to her dresser, peeled off her T-shirt and reached in until she found the peach silk teddy. She slipped it on, discarding her bikini underpants. The one good thing about her hectic life, it kept her slim.

When she came back to bed, Burt handed her a glass.

"I remember the first champagne we ever shared."

He was smiling.

She took a sip. "At the Seventh Street Bistro, remember?"

"I remember."

Her brain still felt fuzzy, because she thought she saw something floating in the glass.

"Burt?"

"Fish it out." He was grinning.

The ring was exquisite. Five tiny diamonds on a white platinum band.

"This Sunday. Five years."

She was speechless for a moment, then blurted out, "I have a surprise for you, too. I talked to Alice, and she's agreed to take care of the kids over the weekend. I booked us a room at the Sheraton."

"I like the way you operate."

"It's kind of a present for both of us, but I didn't think you'd mind."

"I love you, Sandy. I want you to know how much I've appreciated the past five years."

"Me, too. Now drink your champagne," she said softly.

He looked at her, puzzled by the abrupt change of subject.

"According to my calculations, Mr. Savage, we have less than two hours before one of the little savages gets home. I'd like to put that time to the best possible use."

"I'm going to make sure you take naps more often."

She was laughing as he took her in his arms.

Harlequin American Romance

COMING NEXT MONTH

#233 GUARDIAN ANGEL by Cathy Gillen Thacker

Jason O'Leary was going to be the father of her baby. The plan was simple—Carlys would raise the child she'd always wanted, while Jason would act as advisor, protector and emotional support. But when Carlys became pregnant, she noticed that her guardian angel was a flesh-and-blood man—and the simple plan turned complex.

#234 MARRY SUNSHINE by Anne McAllister

A bungled divorce wasn't funny—so why was Austin Cavanaugh laughing? Clea didn't find humor in discovering that the marriage she thought had ended seven years ago was never dissolved. But then Austin announced that he liked being married and intended to stay that way. This time he carried the joke too far.

#235 TELL ME A STORY by Dallas Schulze

Dr. Ann Perry was seeing a whole new side to her neighbor, Flynn. The irresponsible bon vivant had become the model parent since he'd found a homeless little girl. He was great at bedtime stories, terrific at reassuring a lost and lonely child that her parents would soon come to claim her. He had easily won the child's trust, but in so doing, would he win Ann's love too?

#236 WILDFLOWER by Julie Kistler

The zany Wentworth sisters were in the news again—this time it involved Jo. Neil knew from local gossip that she was unique and that his investigation would be difficult—especially when he had to lie to the most trusting woman ever put on God's green earth....

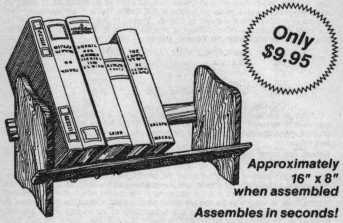

"GIVE YOUR HEART TO HARLEQUIN" SWEEPSTAKES
OFFICIAL RULES
NO PURCHASE NECESSARY TO ENTER OR RECEIVE A PRIZE

1. To enter and join the Preview Service, scratch off the concealment device on all game tickets. This will reveal the values for each Sweepstakes entry number, the number of free books you will receive, and your free bonus gift as part of our Preview Service. If you do not wish to take advantage of our Preview Service, only scratch off the concealment device on game tickets 1-3. To enter, return your entire sheet of tickets.

2. Either way your Sweepstakes numbers will be compared against the list of winning numbers generated at random by computer. In the event that all prizes are not claimed, random drawings will be held from all entries received from all presentations to award all unclaimed prizes. All cash prizes are payable in U.S. funds. This is in addition to any free, surprise or mystery gifts that might be offered. Versions of this Sweepstakes with different prizes may appear in other mailings or at retail outlets by Torstar Ltd. and its affiliates. This presentation offers the following prizes:

(1)	*Grand Prize	$1,000,000 Annuity
(1)	First Prize	$25,000
(2)	Second Prize	$10,000
(5)	Third Prize	$5,000
(10)	Fourth Prize	$1,000
(2,000)	Fifth Prize	$10

   . . .*This presentation contains a Grand Prize offering of a $1,000,000 annuity. Winner may elect to receive $25,000 a year for life up to $1,000,000 or $250,000 in one cash payment. Winners selected will receive the prizes offered in the Sweepstakes promotion they receive.

   Entrants may cancel Preview Service at any time without cost or obligation (see details in the center insert card).

3. This promotion is being conducted under the supervision of Marden-Kane, an independent judging organization. By entering the Sweepstakes, each entrant accepts and agrees to be bound by these rules and the decisions of the judges which shall be final and binding. Odds of winning in the random drawing are dependent upon the total number of entries received. Taxes, if any, are the sole responsibility of the winners. Prizes are non-transferable. All entries must be received by March 31, 1988. The drawing will take place on April 30, 1988 at the offices of Marden-Kane, Lake Success, New York.

4. This offer is open to residents of the U.S., Great Britain and Canada, 18 years or older except employees of Torstar Ltd., its affiliates, subsidiaries, Marden-Kane and all other agencies and persons connected with conducting this Sweepstakes. All Federal, State and local laws apply. Void wherever prohibited or restricted by law.

5. Winners will be notified by mail and may be required to execute an affidavit of eligibility and release which must be returned within 14 days after notification. Canadian winners will be required to answer a skill testing question. Winners consent to the use of their name, photograph and/or likeness for advertising and publicity in conjunction with this and similar promotions without additional compensation. One prize per family or household.

6. For a list of our most current prize winners, send a stamped, self-addressed envelope to: WINNERS LIST c/o MARDEN-KANE, P.O. BOX 701, SAYREVILLE, N.J. 08872.

SWPS-1B

Harlequin Intrigue
Adopts a New Cover Story!

We are proud to present to you
the new Harlequin Intrigue cover design.

Look for two exciting new stories each month, which
mix a contemporary, sophisticated romance with the
surprising twists and turns of a puzzler . . . romance
with "something more."